Real Tales of Surf Arcana

# A PERFECT WAVE

Real Tales of Surf Arcana

# A PERFECT WAVE

J.B. RAFFERTY

For information contact;
Address
www.jbrafferty.com

Book and Cover design by J.B. Rafferty
Back Cover Photo — iStock. by Getty Images

ISBN: 978-0-9966072-0-9
First Edition: August 2015

*To my mermaid-haired angel, Michele, who has been more help than you can imagine and is always there when I need her.*

*And to my parents Joan and John for their life-long encouragment and never giving up on me.*

## Chapter 1

# *Life is a Beach*

Dense fog blurs all lines of this Southern California beach. The locals call it "June Gloom." You might imagine that June Gloom occurs in June, and most years you would be correct, but the real creep factor is that it's now Labor Day, the unofficial last day of summer. Today should be a time to have one last chance to spend an entire day at the beach on a weekday, a time for catching a few last rays, and a time to get mentally and emotionally ready for a new school year.

It is most definitely not a time for June Gloom.

To make matters worse, the surf is flat. It's not even just blown out, it's virtually nonexistent. You would have a better chance of catching a wave in your bathtub, and it's been like this for almost two straight weeks. The feeble lapping of water on the shore isn't even enough to mask the clatter of an occasional shellfish falling from the sky and dropping onto rocks by gulls looking to score a snotty breakfast.

Click.

Clatter.

Slurp.

As happy as a clam one moment, a Happy Meal the next.

Voices are heard somewhere offshore in the thick of the fog. You can just barely make out syllables or an occasional word, but not actual sentences.

"…cannot believe…*something…something…*"

"…waste of time…"

"…freaking grom…"

Despite the lame state of the beach, two surfers sit on their surfboards fifty yards offshore in the impenetrable fog where the visibility is less than ten feet. By the way they are balanced comfortably on their shortboards with the front ends pointing upwards and the back ends under water, it is clear that they are not new to surfing.

The older surfer is aggressively unhappy and declares, "This is exactly why you eat at the loser table."

At seventeen, Dillon Wade has already caught the attention of corporate sponsors. He wears a short wetsuit that protects everything from his elbows to his knees. His cool hazel-green eyes and shoulder-length dirty blond hair make him a poster boy of SoCal cool. And this year, he will be a senior at Dick Dale High School.

Why Dillon Wade is out here surfing with the likes of Torey Kilroy is almost as strange as June Gloom in September.

"I can't believe I let a punk-ass grom like you talk me into paddling out on this puddle at 6 a.m. on the last day of summer."

*The nerd did promise to pay me twenty bills if a perfect wave didn't roll through the fog,* he reminds himself.

"Shh, you'll spook him!" warns the punk-ass grom Torey Kilroy, who is awkward both in appearance and personality. Some might argue that he is a cute kid and has potential, but his sun-bleached hair is sacrificed by a terrible haircut, and his ill-fitting clothes went out of style years ago. Even now his bargain basement board shorts hang so far past his knees they are practically pants. He completes his look with a bright yellow pair of dollar-store shades. To be called a grom at the age of ten or eleven may be fine, but to be called a grom at the age of fifteen is a direct insult.

Torey has always been a quiet, unassuming kid. He is more of a listener than a talker, and extremely shy around girls. But by the end of junior high, he had enough of being one of the invisible kids and decided that things would be different.

Last year he entered high school as a freshman with a new attitude, but he tried way too hard to be cool—his overuse of surfer slang like "dude," and "cool," and "brah" drove his peers to the point of wanting to stick pencils in their ears to avoid hearing him utter those words ever again.

His overzealous efforts to be cool attracted the attention of bullies, particularly two older thugs named Sidney and Simon Pawling. The "Appalling Twins," as they were nicknamed, had put a serious cramp in Torey's efforts to become popular. Despite them, he is still determined to fit in, but has yet to crack the "cool code."

The truth is, Torey doesn't mind being by himself. Being raised as an only child in an isolated beach house by a reclusive mother and eccentric beachcomber father, he always had to find ways to amuse himself. To prove the point, he has spent the past two weeks sitting on a surfboard all alone in a wave-less ocean.

He sits by himself for hours until he becomes mesmerized by the rhythms of the surf, and thinks that if he sits there long enough he can figure out what changed in the ocean to make it wave-less. If the ocean were a violin, Torey might be labeled a prodigy. But the ocean is not a violin and he is labeled a loser.

Dillon looks at him just sitting there in a daze. He punches Torey's shoulder, "Are you messing with me?"

"Ouch! Hey, like chill out Dude. Don't be getting all gangsta brah, it's like, not cool." Typical Torey speak.

A pocket of visibility pushes through the fog. The sudden clarity causes Dillon to shake his head and decide to bail on this scene. "Kilroy, you suck the cool out of Kool Aid."

With that he lies down on his board and paddles for shore. He hopes that maybe it's not too late to climb back into bed and catch another hour of shuteye. Not bothering to look back he adds, "You owe me twenty dollars."

"But dude, you didn't stay long enough to see the wave," Torey calls after him, " The deal was…a perfect wave…it will be here any minute. I guarantee."

Dillon doesn't bother to respond. He just paddles.

"It's not fair, bro, you're leaving too soon."

As if responding to Torey's anguished plea, a large swelling pushes upwards against the surface of the water. It quickly grows outwards like a pimple on the ocean's backside. This is the first movement in the agua all morning. Dillon senses it and glances back at a globe of water growing upward to five, ten, fifteen feet in diameter. White cascades of foam spill down and across its circumference.

Torey rejoices with a shout, "You see! Didn't I tell you?!"

Dillon has never seen anything like this before. This strange ball of water is definitely not normal. He knows enough to keep paddling and to get the hell away from it.

The globe of water pushes outwards until it bursts explosively and a crazed lunatic riding a surfboard spurts airborne with a banshee-like scream, as if spit out from the depths like a bad taste in the ocean's mouth.

The surfer splashes down, straddling a longboard. Water drains from his long, stringy, dark hair and spills down his muscular body. His right hand clutches an antiquated harpoon. Enormous tentacles thrash dangerously close to the dude's board.

Torey calls out to Dillon in a loud whisper, "Dude, what did I tell you?"

Dillon is paddling back and away from this freak show like his life depends on it. He couldn't go any faster if a shark was chasing him.

The surfer stands up on his board as the water rises into a perfect ten-foot high wave. The dark surfer settles into the curl and rushes the wave for all it's worth. As quickly as they appeared, the surfer, the menacing tentacles, and the wave disappear into the fog leaving no trace of the uncanny spectacle that just occurred.

Torey triumphantly blurts out, "That was too cool! What did I tell you, dude? That was awesome! Dillon! Dude?"

Dillon is gone. Dillon is already in waist high water scrambling to get back onto land. He runs, stumbles, and falls, forgetting that the surfboard leash is still strapped to his ankle.

A beachcomber watches with amusement. He laughs humorlessly and calls out, "Ha-ha, smooth move ExLax." And then, "Yo Dillon, is Torey out there with you?"

Dillon eases out of his panic long enough to grab up his board and run off without answering.

Jasper Kilroy shakes his head at Dillon's uncharacteristically un-cool behavior.

Years of patrolling the shoreline have tanned the beachcomber's face like chiseled leather, softened only by blonde and grey stubble. His head is framed by a lion's mane of glorious long locks of dirty blonde hair and his athletic-toned body is camouflaged by loose, threadbare clothing.

Torey's father is ruggedly attractive, but because he tends to talk to himself and have unsettling mood swings, and perhaps because of his unsavory tendency to spit, most describe him as that Creepy Beachcomber Guy. Tourists and the locals alike tend to avoid him, but he does clean up the beach, so there is that.

Jasper continues combing the shoreline looking for debris that has been belched up from the ocean. So far this morning he has found mostly deflated cellophane balloons and plastic cups.

His practiced eyes focus on a tangle of seaweed along the shoreline. Dry as dreadlocks. He grabs it and tears at the ungainly mass until he uncovers a brace of red glass globes that are tangled in aged twine. The red glass has been ground opaque by the persistent groping of the briny Pacific. These are fishing floats that were once used to keep nets afloat, long ago replaced by less costly, plastic versions. Green- and blue-colored globes still occasionally find their way onto the world's beaches, but red ones, red ones are rare. Gold is needed to make the glass red and were more expensive to manufacture. Collectors cherish them.

The Beachcomber frowns at his find like it carries bad mojo. He squints his eyes and looks out into the fog. Surely he should be thrilled with this score and place the red globes into his frayed green duffel bag along with his other treasures, but the Beachcomber is an odd man and he is not at all pleased. He stuffs them into the plastic trash bag and continues his joyless patrol of the shoreline.

* * *

The strange surfer rides out his wave towards shore, milking it into the foam. He jumps off his board into knee-deep water and quickly peers through the fog in all directions, as if he desperately needs to find something. Bubbles break surface all around him as a green and bruise colored tentacle as thick as a man's leg slithers through the surface and wraps around his waist.

The surfer struggles against its sinewy grip. "Just a couple of minutes. I just…" He is pulled abruptly back into the water. "I promised," he yells. "Didn't I promise that I wouldn't leave the water you stupid-"

The rest of his promisingly profane sentence is gurgled out as he is pulled beneath the surface. Another tentacle grabs the surfboard leaving no trace that the surfer stood there just a moment earlier.

* * *

Back in the fog, Torey sits alone and wonders, *where does he go? The dude shows up in the fog every morning to ride one wave and then totally disappears.*

The first time Torey saw the strange surfer, he freaked out just like Dillon did. He even promised himself that he would stay away from the ocean for a while, but he was consumed by curiosity and was knee deep in the water the very next morning. He ventured out a little further each morning for the past week to witness the weird surfer's dramatic appearance and riding of one perfect wave before disappearing. Torey has become accustomed to this spectacle and feels relatively safe, but he considers that Dillon's company may have made him a bit overconfident this time.

He has drifted further offshore than he intended, and decides to head back to shore. He is looking the wrong way as a surfboard fin quietly surfaces behind him and circles him like a shark evaluating lunch. When he finally notices it, he watches in wonder until it disappears below the surface. He is again looking in the wrong direction when the mysterious surfer's head slowly breaks through the ocean's surface.

His chilling sea-blue eyes regard Torey; he has been watching him for days and the surfer appreciates that this one is usually far away from the rest of the herd. He splashes up loudly through the surface. Torey shrieks and practically flails off his board.

For the first time, Torey gets a close look at the surfer. His face resembles water-pruned fingers except for the yellowish tinge, and *what is that green and white crusty stuff in his sideburns?* His intense blue irises float on oyster flesh eyeballs, and he smells like low tide. He wears a short red bathing suit with white stripes that run down from the waistband, and he radiates an unmistaken air of menace.

"Your friend finds it safer to be on land."

Torey stares back wide-eyed, realizing that this dude may be something other than just a fellow surfer. He is suddenly not sure if the mysterious dude is just a bit eccentric like he first thought, or if he could be a psycho, or a zombie, or…or…maybe something worse than a zombie.

"Uh…"

Torey's mouth is dry from nerves and his breathing turns shallow. He suddenly can't help but wonder why it took him this long to realize that he should not be as close to this dude as he now finds himself.

*The guy is wielding a freaking harpoon!*

"I think my dad is looking for me and that octopus is still around here somewhere," Torey mumbles lamely. I'll catch you later okay?" He tries to appear nonchalant, but breaks into an all out dash, furiously paddling with long strokes.

The surfer ignores Torey for the moment. He scans the horizon as if he can see clearly through the fog, sniffs at the salty air before finally returning his gaze to his fellow surfer. He gives Torey the once-over and makes a mental checklist of everything from hairstyle to swimwear to surfboard.

Torey looks back over his shoulder and despite his frantic paddling, he has not moved even one yard away from this dude. The fog can be disorienting, but he should have been at least *some* distance from this guy by now. He stops paddling and wishes he had headed back to shore with Dillon.

"Don't worry about the octopus."

*What the...* Torey is officially freaked out, but despite his fears, he can't help himself from blurting out, "Yo brah, like how do you scarf those boss waves, and what is the deal with that octopotomus? Did you off it, or did it like give you the slip, and like what's with the piece?"

The dark surfer scrunches his face as he tries to interpret the words that just came out of this kid's mouth. Much of that long freaking sentence is full of phrases that he has never heard before, but he has questions of his own, like "Why is your hair cut the same as my Aunt Nell's?" and "Why are you wearing pajamas?" and "Did you buy your little surfboard at a toy store?"

"*What?*"

Torey looks down at his board shorts. They fall past his knees and into the water.

"These are board shorts, dude, they're cool." he counters. "Why are you like, totally old-school? You're dressed like the Endless Summer; the first one, I mean, and why are you greenish?"

The dude doesn't know how to answer that. He has not looked

into a mirror for a long time and did not realize that he is greenish.

They stare at each in dumbfounded confusion. It's as if two different eras have crossed paths in some bizarre time warp. They both ask in unison, "What are you talking about?"

The surfer's mood immediately swings from menacing to lighthearted as he punches Torey's shoulder. "You owe me a Coke."

"Ouch, hey."

Torey rubs away the sting, but he is relieved and encouraged that there is finally something that they both understand. He exhales. He does not feel safe, but at least he has time to stall until he can get back onto the beach.

The surfer extends his hand, "I'm Donovan."

Torey shakes it. "T…t…t…Torey."

He can't help but notice that Donovan has a really strong grip, and that it is an uncomfortably long handshake, and his hand feels like supermarket salmon. He makes a mental note to use a fist bump next time, though there won't be a next time if he can get back ashore again.

Donovan finally releases Torey's hand and says, "I have not heard words spoken in the way that you have uttered them, but they are derived from English. Is this America?"

Torey answers the dude's strange question with an innocent smirk, "Even better, this is California."

Donovan is disoriented. A look of concern creases his forehead. His nose wrinkles as he sniffs the air again.

"Hey, don't look at me," Torey says. He who smelt it dealt it."

The surfer doesn't react to the cheesy joke. His mood has quickly swung and he is no longer cheery. Suddenly he seems confused. Unsure of himself…of everything.

Something is terribly wrong. He wants to say something, or ask something, but…

Donovan hesitates, afraid of what the answer to his next question might be. He finally musters his nerve.

"What…what year is this?"

Torey answers him innocently enough, "It's 2015."

The look of panic in this dude's eyes and the draining of color from his already pale face are beyond frightening as he struggles to do the math in his head.

"Sixteen years?" he gasps, "Or is it sixty eight years?"

He strikes his forehead with the heel of his hand. "I have been trapped in that hell for… for…? This cannot be… it felt like forever, but I was certain that it was only one, maybe two…"

He looks around in all directions for evidence that this is some kind of demented joke. He screams out from torment. The ocean turns choppy as if mirroring Donovan's inner turmoil. White caps form on windblown waves.

Torey cannot follow Donovan's crazy line of thought and stops trying, as he must concentrate on staying attached to his board. He holds on tightly as the condition of the ocean becomes increasingly wild, growing with Donovan's rage. Torey wraps his arms and legs around his board to keep from being washed off. *Where did this storm come from?* He looks to Donovan for answers.

"THAT BITCH!" Donovan roars at the top of his lungs. He stands upright on his board clutching both sides of his head in mental anguish. He screams at nothing and everything at the same time.

Torey is scared, yet he has the presence of mind to wonder how it can be windy and foggy at the same time. He decides that it is Donovan's anger that is having this effect on the water, and that his only chance of not being trashed is to try and calm down Donovan.

"Dude chill out! You can come home with me. My Mom can make fish tacos!"

As soon as the words 'fish tacos' leave his mouth, Torey realizes just how ridiculous he must sound. To his surprise, however, the thrashing of the sea settles down, and the water quickly returns to its unnaturally wave-less state as Donovan regains some of his cool. His rage is momentarily sidetracked by this haphazard thought of fish tacos.

Torey loosens his grip on the board to let his blood pump color back to his white knuckles, but he isn't exactly ready to sit up.

"Fish tacos?"

Torey has never met someone whose mood swings so quickly from one extreme to another. *What if this guy decides to really come home with me? Mom would freak. I mean like who knows what will set this guy off again.*

He hesitates before talking, but really, it is not in Torey's nature to keep his mouth shut. "Dude, a lot has happened the past sixteen years, or did you say sixty eight years?"

Donovan shakes his head, "None of this makes any sense."

"It's okay," Torey says, "we can figure this out. Lets see, have you ever eaten Spicy Chipotle Bar-B-Q Jacked Doritos?"

Donovan looks confused. He doesn't even know what chipotle is let alone... "Doritos? What is Doritos?"

Torey exhales sharply, "Um, I hate to tell you this, but it's probably been sixty eight years. But it's cool. I can catch you up on what you've been missing. All sorts of cool things like Doritos and Toaster Strudels. Shoot, you never even played video games like

World of Warcraft or even the old ones like Pac Man and Donkey Kong. And Ben & Jerry's. Chunky Monkey, dude! And rock and roll, and rap music, and Gangnam Style." He sings the lyrics and keeps the beat by using his board as a drum.

"Stop!"

Torey is too far along his roll to stop. "And you never saw Star Wars, I mean like when you find out who Darth Vader really is, Dude! And the World Wide Web, and…"

"For pities sake, enough!"

Torey stops.

Donovan closes his eyes as if to stop his head from spinning. He needs to fight back the crazy part of his brain that is trying to take control. He cannot afford to lose it completely and scare the kid away at this point, though the kid is not as afraid as he probably should be. He goes over it once more in his mind to convince himself that he made the right choice with this Torey. *Torey is a loner, which is good. He spends all his time in the ocean, which is good. He does not shut up, which is annoying, but time is short.* Donovan decides to stick with the plan. He opens his eyes.

As soon as Donovan's eyes open Torey starts talking again, "C'mon, we'll go ashore and I'll buy you an energy drink. Energy drinks are good."

Donovan puts up both hands to prevent Torey from gaining momentum for another tirade. He says, "I cannot step on land."

Torey doesn't get it, "Sure you can. It's right over there."

"Look dude," using Torey's favorite word for emphasis, "A mermaid that I fell in love with all those years ago deceived me. She tricked me. She promised that our love would be eternal. But she only meant to condemn me to serve her sentence in an undersea hell. It has taken me all this time to create a portal that offers a brief respite at the ocean's surface."

Torey scratches his head, "But you have legs."

"The beast that you saw harassing me on the wave is my jailor so to speak." Donovan tells him, "I was able to convince it that it was not my place to be in hell. We have come to agree that it is guarding the wrong prisoner and that it will allow me a chance to find the mermaid who rightfully belongs there. It will not allow me out of the water and out of its reach. It will not trust me to walk on land because it knows that I would never come back. It is a demon charged only with guarding a prisoner. Losing its prisoner would not bode well for it." His stare is a mile away.

Torey can't help but ask, "The octopus talks?"

"No the octopus doesn't talk. What is wrong with you?"

"But? How do you know...?"

Donovan says, "It is difficult to explain, but I must get the mermaid back into the ocean. Only then will I get the chance to set things right."

Torey attempts to follow Donovan's crazy story, "But you said it's been like sixty years, she could be anywhere, like Kansas, or Denver, or..."

"No, even in human form, a mermaid cannot exist beyond sight of the sea. She is in many ways as much a slave to the ocean as I am."

"Okay, but there is a lot of shoreline in the world. She could be anywhere. She might not even be alive anymore."

"Kid, let me tell you about mermaids. Mermaids live for countless hundreds of years. They don't age, and they can take care of themselves, with or without their pagan magic. Boy, I have been searching for a lot longer than I ever realized, but this is the first place that I have ever caught the scent of her intoxicating aroma."

He inhales deeply.

"She is close." He turns his gaze to Torey and says, "Kid, I need your help."

Torey feels strangely flattered, but can't imagine what kind of help he could offer this dude. And really, he does not want to help him. He only wants to figure out how to ditch this psycho and get back home. *Mermaids. As if.* So in order to stall for time he plays along and asks, "What kind of help do you need?"

Donovan lays it out, "Nothing too difficult I assure you. I need you to help me locate the mermaid in her human form and to get her to step into the water. Once in the water, she will regain her mermaid form, and I will drag her back to my hell where she belongs and I will regain my freedom."

"That sounds kind of hard," Torey says. He knows that Donovan is out of his mind crazy, but he does seem to be able to create some pretty sweet waves, even in flat water, and that is way cool. He bluffs, "Maybe if you could show me how to create a perfect wave...?" He knows full well that he is asking the impossible.

Donovan is keenly aware of Torey's hesitation and that he is only just trying to humor him, but he really does need help and will have to sweeten the deal so that he can set the hook firmly before reeling the kid in. He understands immediately what he must offer this young guppy to do his bidding. "A perfect wave?" He pauses for dramatic effect. "Then we shall strike a bargain. Not only will I teach you to create the perfect wave, but I will teach you to be," he milks the moment, "cool."

Torey's eyes widen as he whispers, "You can make me cool?"

Donovan flashes his not-so-pearly-whites.

*How cool would it be to like, be cool?*

He restates the arrangement, "So our deal will be, you help me find the mermaid and I will teach you to create a perfect wave and be cool beyond your wildest dreams." He extends his hand, "Do we have a deal then?"

As tempting as it sounds, there is no way that Torey is going to make a deal with this weirdo. "Um. I need to think about it first. Can I get back to you tomorrow morning?"

Donovan stares him down. He was not expecting the kid to hesitate. His mind reflexively shifts to anger, but he manages to control it. A dead body at this point would attract unwanted attention. "Have it your way," he says, but the deal ends tomorrow morning. If I do not hear from you I am sure that there will be others that would jump at the opportunity to control water."

Donovan never blinks as he and his old wooden longboard along with his harpoon sink slowly beneath the water and out of sight.

Torey exhales sharply and paddles back to shore where it is safe.

## Chapter 2

# *Like, Don't Be A Hater, Dude*

The beachcomber calls out his son's name, "Torey. Torey." He considers that either the fog is too dense for his voice to penetrate or that Torey is already back home. He tries one last time, "Eggo waffles, boy."

Mr. Kilroy finally gives up and heads off across the sand towards the Pacific Coast Highway. He deposits the plastic bag of trash that he collected during his beachcombing into the nearest trashcan and moves on. It isn't five strides later that he turns and goes back for the red glass fishing floats and stuffs them irritably into his duffel bag. He walks past a strip mall of art galleries, restaurants, and a high-end realtor before heading left onto a side street next to a jewelry store.

Dana Point is a beach town that lies between two tourist destinations, Laguna Beach and San Juan Capistrano. To most tourists, Dana Point is merely a pleasant drive along the Pacific

Coast Highway on the way to some place else, and that is exactly how the locals like it. Wrought iron and wooden staircases spill down rocky cliffs that are lush with succulent vegetation and colorful flowers leading to the beach.

Dana Point is a community of sun worshippers and surfers. Many of the people who reside here live the stereotypical laidback, Bohemian lifestyle. Tanned and toned. Cool and trendsetting. It is not a place where you might expect anything to be strange or out of the ordinary or arcane. But here you have it; summer in paradise this year has been drastically less than perfect due to the Gloom.

Jasper Kilroy is a leftover from a tougher era. He strides past the fine shops and cuts through a tightly overgrown alley, and heads straight for a less than modest dive bar that sits out of sight from the leisure class. The pub's battle-scarred sign, having been salvaged from the nose cone of a World War II B17 Flying Fortress, reads "Pair O' Dice." Under the lettering sits a crude painting of a pinup girl riding a bomb, a pair of fuzzy dice dangling from her fingers.

He absentmindedly runs his fingers across the line of bullet holes that cut through the pinup's midriff as he enters the Pair O' Dice Pub. It is pronounced "Paradise Pub." It takes a moment for his eyes to adjust to the dark interior. Dim light from lamps made from once-living blowfish are insufficient to properly illuminate the place.

Kilroy reaches into his satchel and digs out a couple of surfboard fins that he grabbed up during his walk along the shoreline. "More fins," he announces to the empty room as he deposits them into a barrel full of more of the same.

"Not many of those things lately, but leave it to you to find them," a gravelly voice replies.

Kilroy turns to the direction of the voice, but sees only the carved Tiki idol that supports one end of the bar. Two gnarled hands appear on the lip of the bar and pull up a crusty-looking old man who then swings his legless body onto a perch behind the bar.

"A keg line needed cleaning," he explains.

Gunny York has been the proprietor of the Pair O' Dice Pub since his midnight checkout at the V.A. Hospital back in the summer of 1949. This was as far as he got that night; he fell asleep at the doorway, signed the lease for it the next day, and has been here ever since.

"Have you found anything else on your patrol, Jasper?" he asks while he tests the tap by pouring a pint of beer. He slides the pint to Jasper.

"It's five o'clock somewhere," he says.

Kilroy takes a seat on one of the butt-polished leather bar stools. He pushes the beer aside and fishes out the brace of red glass fishing floats from his duffel bag and displays them on the yellowed polyurethane surface of the bar. Gunny lets out a gasp of appreciation.

"Damn," he says, "These things never fail to remind me of Guadalcanal. Remember they used to wash up all over the beach. Great souvenirs to send back home until they started booby-trapping them with mines. The last thing I remember is you pulling me out of the drink despite my screams to be put down and let me die. You remember that day?"

Jasper does not respond. He is used to the old barkeep mistaking him for his father.

Gunny catches himself, "You'd think I would know better by now, but the longer I know you, the more you become the spittin' image of your old man." He adds, "It's like I'm talking to my old partner every time you come in."

Jasper responds, "I didn't know him much."

"Yeah well we was always too busy looking for arcane paraphernalia before Tojo or the Nazis or every other would be stinking world leader could get their filthy hands on it. That magical crap had a high price on the black market, and our government paid us double that to collect it."

He mentally brushes the cobwebs from his memory and adds; "Look at me making excuses for that son of a bitch. Fact of it is, your old dad was the most mean-spirited and nastiest sod I ever met, and I apologize for confusing you with him."

Jasper is uneasy with this conversation and is glad when two young surfers wander in. One of them keeps a suspicious eye on the Beachcomber and the barkeep as the other one rummages through the fin barrel. Once he finds a fin that he likes, the two of them bolt back out the door without so much as a thank you.

"Ungrateful little bastards," Gunny mumbles. "I suppose it was The Nam that chiseled you into the spitting image of your old man."

"Maybe so," responds Kilroy.

"Who knows, maybe your own son Torey will turn out to resemble the both of you. Strapping young lad."

Kilroy snorts back an unkind laugh. "We'll have to see about that. The smart money is on a somewhat softer version."

Gunny studies his friend. He wants to say something, but decides to mind his own business as far as Kilroy's family is concerned.

Kilroy catches Gunny's odd look, and despite his being tired of this conversation, he doesn't let it drop. "What?"

"I was just wondering why the son of a line of war heroes is soft and doesn't know a lick about fighting. It just doesn't seem right."

Kilroy pushes his beer mug forward. "So it's on me?"

Kilroy admits to himself that maybe Gunny might have a point and that he could at least try to teach Torey a couple of fighting moves.

Doing his best to change the subject, Gunny says, "Still, those red floats are a rare find in this time of the world."

* * *

It is about 10:30 a.m., and the beach is no longer lifeless. Beachgoers claim their turf with blankets and towels as the sun's rays burn through the last of the fog.

Torey pulls his board from the water and is happy to step safely back on land. He is not happy with the thought of giving up surfing for a while, but there is no way that he can go back into the water and take the chance of running into that freako Donovan again. *Creating a perfect wave would be cool, but really how could he teach me that,* and *if there really was a mermaid why would she be on land? None of his ridiculous story makes any sense.* And *that dude's temper is like uncool.* Torey is so lost in thought that he doesn't see Dillon approaching.

Dillon rushes him with two hands to his chest and knocks him back into the water. "What the hell was that, twink?" Dillon demands.

Torey scrambles to get back onto his feet. "Wait! What? Hey chill. Why did you run away like a..."

He catches himself from saying something really foolish, but that unfortunate half comment only serves to make Dillon yell louder and become even angrier.

"Like a what? Like a what? What are you trying to say, you little twink?"

Torey suddenly realizes with dismay that Dillon is not alone. Sidney and Simon Pawling are right there with him.

The Appalling Twins! The Appalling Twins are natural-born bullies. They are not identical twins, but each is fifty percent body builder, fifty percent ignorant, and one hundred percent B-hole. They are always up for a fight and never miss a chance to torment stragglers from the schoolyard herd. They are drawn to a fight like sharks to chum, and they are more than delighted to egg Dillon on with inane taunts.

"You ran away?"

"Dude called you out, brah."

"You need to set this right."

Torey turns and rushes for deeper water, but Dillon, who is out-of-his-mind freaked out by the episode with the creepy surfer, is going to satisfy his recent cowardice on the only witness to the event. He grabs Torey by the waistband of his board shorts and hauls him back out of the water wedgie-style. He pushes Torey into Sidney who in turn pushes him at Simon. All three push him back and forth all the way up the beach until they reach the volleyball nets.

Dillon finally shoves Torey down onto the sand so that his wet body gets coated like Shake'n Bake. Every teen in the vicinity is already keenly aware of Torey's plight. They crowd around like seagulls to an unattended open bag of chips.

It is only a gaggle of goth kids who don't rush over for a better vantage point. They watch from the safety of a shady and cool cement wall by the refreshment stand. All of them are dressed to the nines in an excess of black velvet and lace, fishnets and leather, high boots and long gloves. Not the most popular choice for beachwear. Goths do not like to venture out into direct sunlight and risk marring their image, or Heaven forbid, risk tanning their well-preserved pale hides.

A young lifeguard is the only authority-figure on the beach, but because of past run-ins with Sidney and Simon, he adjusts his glasses and continues to scan the empty shoreline just in case someone is in need of saving.

Torey is both winded and confused. His voice cracks with a pained, "Why?"

His innocent plea is enough to cause Dillon to suddenly become aware of his own behavior. He quickly tones it down and snaps out of his fit of rage. He is actually ashamed of himself. He exhales sharply and pulls himself together, but warns Torey, "Just don't ever mess with me like that."

He adds more quietly to Torey, "I thought for sure you were dead meat, you dumbass."

He walks away, still very shaken by the incident, but he has the sense to realize that he is being very uncool by taking it out on Torey.

Torey watches him leave with a sigh of relief. He gets back up thinking he will go back to retrieve his board, but the Appalling Twins have something else in mind. Simon pulls him back by his waistband and sneers.

"We are just getting started, twink."

They both grin evilly and proceed to give him a classic wedgie.

"I don't have a fight with you. Dillon said that it's over," Torey pleads.

Sidney presses his face right up into Torey's grill. "It's over when I say it's over."

"Cut it out you stupid Kooks," Torey retorts, unable to help himself. Kook is another surfer term for a clueless beginner.

The twins exchange glances, as if sharing one brain.

"Atomic Wedgie!" They shout together and haul him up brutally and hang him by the band of his shorts onto the tie-off hook high up on the volleyball post.

Torey squirms, squealing in pain and humiliation. Alarmed by the unbearable strain on his jellies, he flails his legs helplessly as he tries frantically to get off the hook.

To be fair, many of those who have crowded around to witness this unfortunate event unfold wince at Torey's plight. But they know better than to try to help him. *Better him than me*, they think.

"Get used to it grom, we ain't done with you," hisses Simon, "Your day ain't over yet."

Sidney turns to the crowd of teens. "Not a one-a-you dare to let the twink down or you'll be hanging' right up there next to him."

"That's not a threat, that's a promise," Simon adds.

Not one person dares to help Torey, but Torey uses the twins' distraction with the onlookers to press his feet against the post to try to steal a moment of sweet relief. Simon sees what he is up to and sucker punches him right in the gut to discourage the attempt.

Incredibly, one of the female goths steps out from the shade by the concession stand and into the direct sunlight. It is rare that sunshine ever gets its chance to caress this lovely vixen's creamy white flesh.

Her name is Cassandra.

Cassandra is five-nine, slight of build, and has long glorious locks of jet-black hair that contrasts with her perfect ivory complexion. She wears a black ankle-length lace dress with flared long sleeves and a corseted waist.

All eyes turn from Torey to Cassandra. Although an atomic

wedgie does not occur everyday, it is not as rare as witnessing a goth walk unprotected in the sun and risk bursting into flames.

With confident strides, Cassandra walks in her stiletto-heeled boots across the sand towards Torey and his tormentors. She grabs a white plastic chair along the way and drags it with her. She marches defiantly past the Appalling Twins and sets the chair up beneath Torey's feet.

Torey's relief is immediate, but he would rather hang there all day than have Cassandra see him like this. He struggles to unhook his shorts, which have become twisted on the hook.

As far as Sidney and Simon are concerned, she needn't say a word.

The twins are taken aback and stare at her with dumbfounded expressions. They were not expecting someone to actually confront them.

"I thought you like your meat tender, freak," Sidney blurts out.

Cassandra pulls down her shades just enough to stare directly at Sidney with her striking emerald-green eyes.

Sidney doesn't like it when people give him direct eye contact. It makes him self-conscious. It makes him angry. It makes him want to break things. But Sidney does not act out on his anger because he feels insecure around pretty girls. And pretty bloodsucker-looking she-devil girls especially intimidate Sidney Pawling.

Everyone knows that there is no way that Sidney is going to hang her on the pole next to Torey. But Sidney needs to save face. "Show's over losers," he tells the crowd. "Bring your lunch money to school tomorrow."

He makes a special point to threaten Torey, "See you in school, tool."

Sidney and Simon leave the scene laughing and pushing at each other playfully, trying to hide the fact that a girl intimidated them.

Torey finally frees himself with a rip to his shorts and sprawls face down onto the sand. He immediately rolls over and sits back to hide the rip. Although the sand is hot on his exposed right butt cheek, it is the cheeks on his face where he feels the warm rush of blood and the burning sting of humiliation.

For the first week of school, Cassandra will be asked why she took it upon herself to help someone like Torey. Cassandra will just respond with her patented get-out-of-my-face-you-insignificant-creep stare.

Torey stares down at the sand. "Thanks," he mumbles.

Cassandra waits for a flicker of eye contact before offering him a sympathetic smile.

"No problem."

She turns and strides back to join her confused friends at the shady side of the concession stand.

Humiliated, Torey makes his way down the beach to retrieve his board. What a way to end the last day of summer break.

## Chapter 3
## *Not Too Cool For School*

The next morning, Torey would like nothing better than to be carrying a surfboard, but he's now carrying a backpack. Instead of board shorts, he wears cargo shorts and a belt. A short-sleeved button-down shirt covers his suntanned torso. And for the first time since June, he sports sneakers and socks!

His humiliating wedgie is still in the forefront of his mind. At one point during his mostly sleepless night, he talked himself into believing that he has nothing to lose by seeing what Donovan can do to make him cool. Donovan said that he had until this morning to make the deal. He had no intention of doing so yesterday, but now that he changed his mind he is unable to meet Donovan's deadline because he has to go to school.

He took the long way to the bus stop along the shore. He was half expecting the surf to have returned, if only as some kind of cosmic kick-in-the-butt, but no, hardly a ripple.

The Gloom is thick. "I don't remember if I mentioned it, but today is the first day school," he calls out, hoping for a response.

Nothing.

Torey briefly considers ditching school, but he has never ditched before.

He calls into the fog. "I can't miss the first day of school!"

Still there is no sign that Donovan may have heard his lame excuse. "Okay, well… I'll catch you later, okay?"

Torey turns away from the ocean to mope his way back across the sand to catch his bus, wondering if he just blew his chance to accept Donovan's deal. To his surprise, he hears a crash and turns just in time to see water surge twenty feet up the sand. It soaks his feet.

"Dude, my sneakers! That is rude!"

But after the initial surprise, he can't help but snort back a laugh, appreciating the humor of it. He waves to the empty shoreline and hurries off.

\* \* \*

Donovan floats forty yards off shore. Only his head breaks the surface as he watches Torey run off to catch the school bus. He does not like surprises because surprises agitate his mind and rock its already brittle sense of stability. He worries about his short window of opportunity and if he has time for delays like this. He jabbers to himself, "Scuba–scuba–school bus. I didn't know that it was school time. I forgot about school."

He considers that he may as well get some work done and come back later to see if the kid shows up.

\* \* \*

Dick Dale High, home of the Dick Dale Dolphins, is abuzz with the excitement of a new school year. But Torey is not excited. He sloshes toward the front entrance in his still wet sneakers where he will navigate past cliques of surfer boys, jocks, valley girls, skateboard punks, and the smart kids (sometimes called mathletes).

He notices a freshman wandering with unsure steps in an attempt to get his bearings, totally clueless of the torment that bullies will be dispensing on him soon. Torey was actually hoping that, as a sophomore, he would be exempted from the daily ritual of humiliation and torment. But after yesterday, all such hopes have been dashed.

Torey should know better, but he tells himself that it has been a long summer, and maybe things have changed. He flashes a Hawaiian Shaka hand sign to his fellow surfer dudes, thumb and pinky finger out with the three middle fingers folded in. "Yo brahs."

Maybe they didn't hear him.

He continues past a group of senior jocks. "Go Dolphins!"

No reaction. They don't have time for anyone who is not a senior or at least a jock.

Torey stares his way awkwardly past a group of attractive mean girls. They mock his tongue-tied gape and salute him with thumbs and forefingers forming capital Ls on their foreheads. He rushes on to escapes their painful giggles. *Maybe it would be better to stay invisible.*

He nods to the guys that he eats lunch with at the dork table, but none return the gesture. They learned the hard way that Torey cannot resist responding to bullies' taunts, which only makes things worse for himself *and* everyone around him. They understand that he does it as a way to hold onto his last shreds of dignity, but they have decided that they will not risk giving

Torey another chance to get them all involved in another Jell-O shampoo episode.

Torey slips back into his shy wannabe persona and shrinks back towards invisibility. He grasps for hope by remembering that Donovan will help make him cool, but how long will that take? *If I can't be cool in high school, then what's the point?* He is painfully aware of his closing window of opportunity.

The goths hang out inside the school lobby, just out of reach of the offending morning sunshine. A high-ranking member of their group, Byron Toomey, is dressed like a Matrix version of a vampire. He wears a long black trench coat and dark shades as he holds court with his fellow brethren, showing off his gloriously expensive new fangs. Faux fangs created by a real dental technician.

"I was going to go with the permanent implants," he embellishes, "but they said I should try these out first to see if I could get used to eating with them. It set me back a grand because these are almost as expensive as the actual implants." He stops his monologue to wipe a spatter of drool off of his lower lip when he notices Torey staring at Cassandra.

Cassandra is Byron's best friend and he will not stand for an outsider like Torey trying to get too close. He gets up into Torey's face trying to startle him with his fangs. Torey only sees Cassandra.

"You don't like the new look?"

Torey doesn't quite get what Byron is talking about, so replies, "That's not a new look, she is always beautiful."

Cassandra's eyes widen as she overhears Torey's comment. She feels her cheeks flush.

Byron is miffed about not getting his desired reaction to his toothy grin. He dismisses Torey with, "You got enough pity from us yesterday. Be gone you stupid meat puppet."

Cassandra steps forward. She is already bored with Byron's new teeth. "Leave him alone Byron. You could very well be in his shoes if your mother didn't spawn a six foot three freak of nature. And we are not vampire kids, by the way. We are goths."

Torey seizes the moment, "I just want to say thanks for, you know, yesterday, and well…" he stalls.

She helps him out. "Maybe some day you can return the favor." Cassandra's smile reveals just how stunningly attractive she has become in the past few years.

Byron makes a rude gagging sound. "I just threw up in my mouth a little."

Cassandra silently gestures to Torey with her emerald eyes that it might be a good time to move along. Torey wanders off with the daze of a boy who suddenly realizes that he has a serious crush on a beautiful girl.

Byron loudly warns Cassandra with light-hearted melodrama, "Watch yourself girl or you will find yourself cast out to dwell with the suntan oil bimbos and valley girls."

Torey turns as he overhears Byron's remark and has the strange urge to defend Cassandra's honor, but is uncomfortable by the way that Byron is staring him down. Torey looks quickly down at a sheet of paper to check for his homeroom number. *Who am I kidding? I am in exactly the same boat as I was last year, except maybe worse. I am still a stupid outcast and there is no way that the first day of school could get any worse.*

Just then, Dillon brushes past him and says quietly, "I overreacted yesterday. We cool?"

Torey glances back, but Dillon is gone before he has a chance to respond. As he turns back, he bumps right into someone.

"Top of the morning, twink." Sidney immediately puts Torey

in a headlock and growls menacingly. "Where's the lunch money?" Sidney tightens the headlock and repeats, "Where's the lunch money, twink?"

Torey squirms against Sidney's grip. Sidney laughs and tightens the headlock as Simon rifles through Torey's backpack. Students quickly gather to get a better view. They are eager for some action before homeroom on the first day of school.

Simon pulls out a sandwich and holds it up for all to see. "The twink thought that he could get away without coughing up his lunch money because his *mommy* made him a *sammy*." He unwraps the tin foil to reveal sardines on white bread. He wrinkles his nose.

"You sick mother!" He throws the offending sandwich against a locker.

"You were told to bring your lunch money," Sidney reminds him. Simon pulls a juicy peach from Torey's backpack.

"I don't have lunch money," Torey struggles against Sidney's sweaty armpit, and adds, "You stupid b-holes."

A voice from the crowd, "Oh no."

"You know smart guy," Simon says, "we was gonna let you go easy, but now…"

He doesn't need to finish his thought; his brother knows exactly what he is thinking. He grins evilly and holds the peach up like a trophy for all to see.

"That b-hole comment is gonna cost you." Simon pulls back the waistband of Torey's pants for emphasis.

Torey struggles and pleads with them to, "Knock it off."

Simon mimics him with an exaggeratedly whiney, "Knock it off!" And then he does something that will make him infamous in the history of schoolyard bully-dom. He slam-dunks the peach down Torey's pants.

Sidney laughs wickedly as he pulls up on Torey's whites and grinds the ripe peach home.

"OH!" The crowd exclaims.

"A PEACH WEDGIE!"

"This is *epic!*"

Torey is humiliated to the brink of tears, as the soft ripe fruit is smushed home. He can already feel juice running down his legs. Simon pushes him into the brace of lockers for good measure and high fives Sidney. The bell rings to end Round One and to signal that it is time for homeroom.

Torey slides down a locker as the crowd disperses. He is in his own private hell and doesn't dare to look up to see if Cassandra was there to witness his second wedgie in two days. He tries to convince himself that she missed the whole event.

And the first day of school has officially begun.

* * *

A mile off the coast and a thousand feet below the surface lays an eight-foot wide portal on the ocean's floor. It is an entrance to a hellish dimension that shimmers like liquid metal and is framed by a random tangle of twisted steel. Upon closer inspection it resembles a crude representation of what surely must be a long forgotten alphabet or an alchemist's runes. Most of the symbols are bonded together while others float on their own accord defying the very laws of physics. A duplicate of the intricate frame is mirrored on the underside of the portal. A visible charge of energy flickers eerily as it runs a haphazard course along the symbols both above and below the entrance.

Inside, Donovan's miserable existence in hell continues amidst a mind numbing pounding. The cavernous space reverberates like an irregular heartbeat. A disconcerting red glow pulses from every nook and cranny of this underwater abyss. This is not underwater as in under the Pacific off the coast of California; it is a different dimension entirely. Donovan's only escape is through the portal that he managed to create during his long incarceration.

This place is unlike anything that exists on an Earthly plane. It is a virtual graveyard of wooden and steel ships in all stages of corrosion and rot. Merchant vessels and pirate schooners are scattered and partially buried everywhere, cluttered with a spectacular array of rubbish that represents a wicked collection of loss due to recklessness, bad luck, and wanton destruction. Broken masts and gaping holes are a recurring theme.

Once your eyes adjust to the eerie low light your focus might shift to enormous stone pillars with ornate carvings that could only come from a place like Atlantis or some other doomed and long-forgotten society. These finely carved artifacts are wildly contrasted by hundreds of decaying Polynesian Tiki poles that jut up at disheveled angles with their brutish warrior faces pleading for sunlight.

Countless human skeletons and bones drift along the floor, along with all sorts of bottles, guns, swords, trinkets, and every man-made object that could possibly be lost at sea. Green, blue, yellow, and red glass fishing floats are tangled everywhere on tattered sails pulling eternally upward against age-weakened twine like alien pods in some extreme science fictional garden. Occasionally a group of glass floats will break their bonds and float upwards in a brash attempt to escape this place that is surely a monument to man's misfortune.

No fish swim these waters. No crabs crawl atop the dead coral. The only sign of life is a giant octopus that lurks within the shattered hull of an old frigate atop a pile of gold and silver coins and spent ammo casings; its tentacles coil relentlessly on themselves.

The only other movement in this wretched place is Donovan toiling away despite the mind-numbing pulsing of red. No air spills from his nostrils. He wishes often that he would simply die from lack of oxygen, but hell will not let him off that easy. Hell is not a place for dying; hell is a place for paying the price for past evil misdeeds. By the looks of this place, Donovan's double-crossing mermaid had a serious debt to pay.

Donovan was confused and tormented when he first awoke here, but one thing in his mind was clear: *once everything is put in place and order has been achieved, his time here will be over.* He grabs the skeleton of a Japanese fighter pilot and places the bones gently and carefully alongside those of others long dead.

Everywhere debris and remains are stacked in neat, orderly piles. Pyramid-shaped stacks of skulls, piles of meticulously ordered bullets and torpedoes, neatly arranged rows of torn and tattered flags. Donovan has spent years attempting to compel a sense of order and reason amidst the chaos, but there is so much disorder that it would take an army a hundred years to complete the task. Donovan wearily looks for another skeleton to arrange with the others. Fatigue shows in his eyes with every pulse of the red glow. He gives in to exhaustion and loses consciousness.

A carved figurehead of a mermaid on the prow of a ship seemingly stares down at Donovan. Hair moves as her head shifts. This is no figurehead carved from ancient wood. This is an honest to God living mermaid. Her timeless beauty contrasts in this place like a gem in a coal pile. Unfortunately the red light that illuminates her high cheekbones and almond shaped eyes makes her look like an angry she-demon. She kicks her tail softly and glides down slowly towards the unconscious Donovan.

Her face echoes a look of despair and pity as she studies

Donovan's face carefully. She knows that everything would be much easier if she could communicate with him, but a mermaid needs to bond with a man before she can speak his language. Donovan had already bonded with a mermaid and look where that got him. He will not allow that to ever happen again. But it is important to her, so she will try once again.

She contours her body to maneuver it as close to his as she can without actually touching him. She wants his body to slowly become accustomed to hers. She doesn't want him to become consciously aware of her presence, but her soft cheek accidentally brushes ever so slightly against his stubble and scar battered cheek.

Donovan starts awake with a scream of panic and rage. His arms strike out reflexively to protect himself. The mermaid deftly dodges his blow and his fist slams into a pile of skulls that scatter into disorder. This outburst causes the eerie red light to glow brighter and the pulsing to thrum louder, much like the way the ocean responds to his anger.

Donovan looks about frantically as if waking for the first time in this forsaken place. He gradually gets his bearings, but yells once more for no apparent reason; perhaps to intimidate, but more likely to relieve pent up torment that was created from the terrible place. He clutches at his head to fight the pain and forces himself to continue to rearrange the pile of skulls back to order until the infernal throbbing subsides.

The mermaid darts back to the safety of the wreckage as two other mermaids bolt quickly from their hiding places ready to protect her.

* * *

That afternoon after school, Torey grabs his board and anxiously paddles into the surf, fearing that Donovan will not be there. He is relieved when he finally sees him out in deeper water, waiting for him.

They shake on the deal and Donovan celebrates by creating a sweet wave for Torey to surf. Torey momentarily forgets his distressing first day of school as he cuts up the face of the wave. He catches air with a wild spray of foam, sticks the landing and rides it until it peters out leaving nothing but a ripple to lap the shore. A wave that no one but Torey and Donovan ever knew existed.

They are far out in deep waters where waves do not naturally break and are out of sight from inquisitive eyes. Donovan sits on his board and creates wave after unnatural wave for Torey to surf. "Damn, but that is some wild surfing you kids do these days," he exclaims with excitement, "I am going to have to give one of those baby boards a try."

"Shortboards," Torey corrects him.

"How's that?"

"It's a shortboard, alright?"

Torey's humiliating day at school was too overwhelming to thoroughly enjoy the rush of surfing. "What's the point?" he mumbles and slouches down on his board.

"Kid, you just caught a nice wave. Where is your enthusiasm? What's your issue?"

"But nobody saw it, I mean…"

Donovan regards him with his bloodshot pale blue eyes in a way that gives Torey a skin-crawly feeling. He waits for Torey to continue; instead he breaks eye contact and looks down.

"Alright kid, out with it. What has gotten your nuts in a cluster?"

Torey looks up sharply, feeling very uncomfortable with the

reference of his nuts being in a cluster. "How am I going to be cool if no one sees me riding these waves?"

"You tell me," Donovan replies, "What is more important: surfing a killer wave or being cool?"

"It's not just that," Torey replies. "I mean wedgies and humiliation are not going to make me cool."

"Kid, I don't always understand much of what you say, but I do understand wedgies."

"You do?" says Torey, hoping for commiseration.

Donavan chuckles, remembering. "Sure, I administered a few wedgies in my day. But it's not like you've gotten the Atomic Wedgie?"

Torey sighs. "Worse."

"Worse? You do understand that the Atomic Wedgie is the one where the waistband is yanked…."

Torey finishes the sentence for him. "…yanked over your head. Trust me, I know."

"Then what could be worse than an Atomic Wedgie?" Donovan asks with eager anticipation.

"I don't want to talk about it," Torey says emphatically.

Donovan pushes. "C'mon kid, it's alright. We will have to get past this obstacle if we are to make you cool, and you need to be cool if we are to find my treacherous mermaid."

Torey's cheeks flush red with shame. He cannot believe that he has to relive and share his worst ever humiliation with Donovan, but he decides to trust him.

"What is worse than an atomic wedgie? It's worse when they drop a peach down there and wedge it up your crack," he blurts out. He looks to Donovan for sympathy.

Donovan takes a moment to form a mental image, then suddenly bursts out with uncontrolled, hysterical laughter. He laughs so hard that he falls off his board and sinks beneath the surface.

Torey sits dejected and alone. He realizes that it was a mistake to trust Donovan, a mistake to hope that he wouldn't laugh at him like the rest of the jerks. *At least now I don't have to hear him laughing at me.*

Bubbles break the surface. Loud guffaws are totally audible.

"It's not funny," Torey yells at the water. He doesn't cry, but is close to it. He shakes his head and slumps his shoulders even lower. The bubbles and laughter begin to taper off as if Donovan could sense his pain. One last tiny bubble pops the surface.

"My homeroom teacher called me Peaches," Torey recalls under his breath. He's at least glad that the worst of his embarrassment is finally over.

Just then, rolls of uncontrollable laughter break the surface with the word "Peaches." It is the sort of outright belly laugh that brings tears to your eyes and uncomfortable glares from those who aren't in on the joke.

Torey can't take it anymore. Despite his best effort to control them, tears spill from his eyes. Tears fueled from a lifetime of not fitting in and the frustration of his recent humiliations. Long-held tears roll down his cheeks. Even this dude, who he thought might be a friend, is piling it on with the rest of them.

"Screw it," he sobs, and for the first time in his life he prefers the covers of his bed to the roll of the ocean. He paddles to shore, intending to never look back.

Torey is so busy wallowing in his own personal pity party; he doesn't realize a wave is coming at him from the wrong direction. It raises him up and carries him strangely away from shore and back towards the jerk Donovan who is still laughing at him. Torey struggles frantically to hold onto his board as he is swept up and over the falls.

Wipe out!

Torey coughs up water and regains his board once again next to Donovan's longboard. "What the hell is wrong with you?" he yells, Do you want to give me a wedgie too? You might as well, you stupid jerk!"

Donovan resurfaces and lays his arms across his board. He shakes his head, "Kid, you need thicker skin."

"I have calluses on my butt!" Torey shouts. "How much thicker does it need to be?"

"Alright, alright I apologize. Though I guarantee that sometime in the near future, you will appreciate the humor of your recent ordeal." One last snicker probably didn't help matters, but Torey has no choice but to listen. Donovan assures him.

"Before you know it, you are going to be too cool for school."

"Gimme a break," Torey says. He looks back to shore.

Donovan reminds him, "We shook on it, remember? Lesson one; always be a man of honor. A man who keeps his word."

*Lesson one?* Torey thinks. *I have kept my word for my entire life and look where I am now.* He says belligerently, "So tell me smart guy, just how do you plan to make me cool?"

"So you do plan on keeping up your part of our bargain, correct?" Donovan asks.

*Was he being serious? It's not even totally likely that mermaids even exist.* Torey just looks at Donovan and does not feel the need to answer him.

"Go back to school and study the 'cool' kids," Donovan says.

"Watch their interaction with the other cool kids, their interactions with the uncool kids, and their interactions with authority figures. Then come back and tell me what they all have in common."

Torey cannot believe that Donovan is actually giving him a homework assignment. "Are you telling me that I still have to go to school?"

"Kid, school is where you are going to practice and hone your skills. School is where you learn things, where you will learn to be cool. Besides, what good is being cool if you are out here by yourself floating on a surfboard? The fishies don't care about cool."

Torey asks suspiciously, "You really think that you can make me cool?"

"Have I ever not told you the truth?" he asks. After a pause he adds, "Just leave the peaches at home for now."

Torey has no way of knowing if Donovan has ever lied to him before, but decides to trust him.

At least for now.

# Chapter 4

## *Lessons Learned*

Torey and his family live in a ramshackle beach house of the sort that you would expect to find on a deserted island. It is built up against a rocky cliff and appears to be constructed from salvaged supplies. "Rickety" is a good way to describe this dwelling: wobbly bamboo stairs lead to an unleveled rooftop deck that is overgrown with flowering vines that reach out from the face of the cliff. A tangled net stretches from the deck to the nearest palm tree creating what looks to be the most dangerous hammock ever.

A windblown dune of sand partially obscures some of the haphazard collection of wood barrels and crates that clutter the yard and what appears to be a boat tied down under a blue tarp. The barrels are full of fishing poles, beach umbrellas, buoys, Tiki torches, shells of all sorts, sunglasses, and car keys. There is even a box filled with lost dentures.

There is a strange sense of order amongst the chaos, yet it is remarkable that this place hadn't been condemned years ago; perhaps the tangled piles of driftwood have camouflaged it from bureaucratic eyes.

Say what you will, but the palm trees around Torey's family's house are perhaps the only coconut bearing palm trees in the entire state of California. Torey's dad does not care much about aesthetics, but the thought of neutered and barren palm trees was an affront to his sensibilities. He made it a point to plant real freaking palm trees that bare real freaking coconuts.

Torey leans his board next to a dozen others in a rack that is built against the side of his house. He notices the barrel full of those weird glass fishing floats that his dad is obsessed with and claims the brace of red ones to hang in his bedroom. He sometimes wonders why his father collects all this stuff, but he is too preoccupied with his recent humiliation to worry about it now. He heads inside for dinner.

It is darker inside than one might expect for a beach house. Heavy curtains cover the windows. The furniture looks as if it was salvaged along with the rest of the junk outside. The décor is reminiscent of a retro sixties pad. Glass jars full of smooth pieces of sea glass are everywhere. Some are filled with white pieces, others with green, or brown pieces of sand etched glass. A couple are even filled with varying shades of blue glass.

His dad the beachcomber waits at the kitchen table. He has set only two places. Torey can smell the over-cooked fish sticks and fries in the oven. He does not like his father's cooking and will never forget the time that he had to eat French fries that were burnt on one end and had freezer frost on the other. "Yuck."

"Where's Mom?" Torey asks. The oven's timer bell dings just in time to save the food from becoming totally inedible.

"She is still not feeling well," his dad answers. "Went to bed early." He pulls a hot tray from the oven and unceremoniously scrapes half the food onto Torey's plate and dumps the rest onto his own.

Torey sneers at his dinner, but is happy that his fries are at least equally burnt from end to end. He is getting used to this cuisine, but really misses his mom's cooking. He has no choice but to douse both the fish sticks and the fries with a heavy dollop of mayonnaise.

His father asks, "Is school alright?"

Torey shrugs and lies. "Yeah, sure."

Jasper studies his gangly son as he chews a bite of sticked fish. "Do you want me to teach you some moves?"

"What do you mean, 'moves?' Like dancing?"

His dad rephrases the question, "Do want me to teach you how to fight?"

"What do you know about fighting?" Torey asks suspiciously.

"Do you know what a Navy Seal is?" his dad asks.

"Yeah, but…"

"Kid, I have been to hell and back and the fact that I am still alive is not on account of my dancing skills. Clean up the dishes and meet me outside."

"Now? I mean, I have homework, and…really you were a Seal?"

"Aside from surfing, do you even exercise?" Jasper asks. "Don't answer that. You do your homework and be ready for a workout tomorrow morning."

Torey stares back dumbly.

"I want twenty pushups and twenty sit ups tonight before you go to bed even if you have to stop and rest in between. And tomorrow you do two sets of each, and so on."

Torey has no intention of starting an exercise regiment. "I could probably do fifty pushups, but it's not fair."

"Fair? If you think I won't know if you slack off you are sadly mistaken. You may not realize when someone is trying to help you, but if you even do one less sit-up than fifty…"

"Fifty?" Torey whines. "But you said…"

"You do less than fifty, and I will give you much worse than a peach wedgie."

Torey is mortified. *How does he know?* There is no sound to make it official, but Torey's self-esteem has just hit rock bottom.

* * *

At 5am the next morning, Torey is dressed to surf and has forgotten about his Dad's threat to teach him how to fight. He only has maybe two hours before the bell for homeroom rings. He pauses to check out one of the new boards his dad acquired. It is a longboard like Donovan's. He considers maybe giving it a try, but decides that it is too heavy to drag down to the beach. He grabs his usual board and as he turns he bumps right into his father. "Oh no," he says out loud, suddenly remembering what his dad said last night.

The beachcomber gives Torey the once over. "Well, you did maybe twenty pushups, I'll give you that."

Torey does not respond. He is anxious to get in the water and it shows. He just wants to talk to Donovan a little more before going to school.

"I was surprised that you are up early and–"

Torey interrupts him, "Well yeah, but I woke up early to…"

His dad finishes the sentence, "Float on a puddle. I made a

vow to teach you to defend yourself, and Sonny Boy, I am going to keep my word."

The Beachcomber slaps his son across the face. Not a hard slap, but enough to sting. Torey drops his board. Shocked, his upper lip begins to quiver.

"Now we can do this all morning, or I can show you how to prevent that from ever happening again."

Torey is confused. He cannot believe that his dad just hit him. His pride or what is left of it is bruised a deep shade of purple, but his curiosity wins out. He snivels, "How can I stop that?"

His father challenges him. "Slap me."

Torey really wants to slap him, but he doesn't have the nerve to. His father sweetens the deal.

"Look at this as being a win-win situation. If you strike me, I will be so damned proud of you, and if you miss, you may just learn something."

Torey considers his situation. "Um…like, I can't like, I mean…"

"If you hit my face I will buy you a car."

Torey's eyes open as wide as hubcaps. *Cars are cool, girls like dudes with cars, and a car will make me cool.*

His dad stands flat-footed with his hands at his sides, and his chin jutted forward. He exhales loudly from impatience.

Torey knows that he is about to deck his father. He counts in his mind, "One…two…" and throws his best right hand uppercut straight at his father's smirking mug.

With lightning like speed, his old man brushes the punch away with his right forearm, sweeps Torey's arm down with his right hand, and strikes ferociously upward with his left elbow to Torey's triceps. He deftly pulls back before actually hurting his son.

Torey is stunned at the speed of what just happened. His mind is freaked out. "Whoa."

His dad smiles. "I am going to teach you how to move your body to exert the maximum amount of force. It will take just one hour of training and you will own this move. With a little more training you will master it. And, if you use it once on a bully in front of an audience, you will never again be on the receiving end of a wedgie. Are you ready for the responsibility of this kind of power?"

Torey has already forgotten that he intended to meet with Donovan this morning. "Heck yeah," he exclaims.

Torey and his dad spend the next hour training with boot camp-like intensity. Torey is winded, but is determined to suffer through it. *If this is what it's going to take to finally be able to maybe stand up for myself and get some respect, then so be it.*

But *why did it take him so long to teach me this?*

\* \* \*

Torey hurries to school. His nerves are on edge. He is overconfident from his first training session with his dad and is running possible scenarios through his mind in case he runs into the twins. He knows that he cannot hope to beat them both, but one of them is going to take a good shot. He has the element of surprise and this is going to be wicked.

Torey pays no attention to the snickering and outright laughter of his classmates as he stands at the intersection of two halls outside his homeroom, now dubbed "Peach Wedgie Way" by the student body. He scans the hallways looking for the Appalling Twins. He will not take the chance of being caught by surprise this time. He concentrates only on what is about to occur and how it might be the first step to dragging his reputation back from the muck.

Dillon does not hate Torey, in fact he still feels badly about how his actions the other day resulted in getting Torey hung up by his board shorts. He can see Torey is tense, and assumes that he is bracing himself for another wedgie. "Relax, they're in detention."

Two emotions immediately flood over Torey: disappointment and relief. He realizes that he wasn't breathing. He sucks in a breath and he heads into homeroom.

Torey slumps into his chair and absentmindedly doodles a picture of Donovan's octopus' tentacles on one of his brown paper bag book covers. His drawing skills aren't half bad.

Torey suddenly snaps out of his mental funk. He thinks, *Donovan. Shoot, I forgot all about him. I hope he isn't angry.* And then he remembers, *he gave me homework, but what was it? That's it, I'm supposed to figure out what the cool kids have in common.* He actually says out loud, "Wow, how could I forget?"

"Forget what?"

Torey looks up to see his homeroom teacher standing in front of him, and he seems impatient. Torey returns a blank stare. The rest of the class laughs at his expense. Mr. Nussman finally says, "Move back one seat, Mr. Kilroy."

Torey asks defensively, "What? Why?"

Mr. Nussman emphasizes each word as if Torey was slow. "Because...we...have...to...make...room...for...our...new... classmate...who...due...to...circumstances...that...will... remain...unspoken...has...gotten...herself...transferred...out... of...her...regularly...assigned...class."

Torey is sick of it all and is too tired to care anymore. "Dude, it's homeroom, nobody cares where we sit."

Mr. Nussman does not appreciate Torey's tone of voice and

becomes more aggravated by the chorus of, "Oooohs," from the rest of the class.

Cassandra peeks at Torey from behind Mr. Nussman. She can't help but grin at Torey's belligerent attitude. Torey finally realizes that everyone was shifting seats in order to make room for her. He jumps up. "Hi Cassandra." Unfortunately in his excitement he stomps on Nussman's foot.

Mr. Nussman loses his cool. "Okay pal, it's detention for you."

Torey quietly stares down Nussman, trying his best not to say something that will get him in more trouble than he is already in. He grabs his books and heads for the door. He smiles weakly at Cassandra. "I warmed the chair up for you." He leaves without further incident.

As the class finally settles down for attendance Torey sticks his head back in and knocks on the door.

"Are you pushing my buttons, Mr. Kilroy?"

"Where is detention?" Torey asks innocently.

* * *

A small plaque on the door reads "Auxiliary Gym," but the students know it as The Little Gym. Or The Old Gym. Or The Gulag.

Inside The Gulag, the gym teacher Chuck Boyle holds court. He is a bulldog of a man with an old school attitude. He stares down a group of five delinquents who slouch on the wood bleachers that have been pulled out from the wall. They are all of the usual misfits.

Mr. Boyle goes through the roll. "Spill it, Johnson."

Johnson is a jock, a real competition junky with a short temper. He is a man-child whose emotional stability has not kept pace with his muscle-toned adult body. "Fighting," he replies.

"Howard?"

Howard, the other jock in the room who is tall and lanky yet deceptively sinewy, replies, "Fighting."

Boyle eyes the two. "Let me guess."

Johnson grins and jabs Howard's shoulder. Howard responds with a slap to Johnson's head. Johnson's eyes go wide with rage.

"Are you kidding me?" Boyle's tone is more than enough to put an end to the ruckus. He motions to the next kid.

Rafael is the only sophomore in a room of seniors. He sports a tank top that shows off a nasty, yet mostly healed, road rash on his right shoulder and upper arm from skateboarding. His rash is a good reflection of his attitude. He says, "Hey, I told Ramirez I would buff out the scuff on her car better than new, but she was all lost in her freak and would not deal with simple reason."

Boyle looks at him. "I don't even speak that jive, but I will take your word for it." Mr. Boyle does not care for Principle Ramirez either.

Next up are Simon and Sidney. He puts his hands up to prevent them from talking. "It doesn't even matter." Mr. Boyle regards the five boys with a frown and considers that it is going to be a long day. But miracles of miracles, the door swings open and Torey steps in. Boyle's frown turns upside down.

"Name and offense," he commands.

"Um, Torey. Torey Kilroy, and, um, I'm not really sure."

The other delinquents find this to be funny. "Way to be, Killjoy," someone calls out.

"Alright, knock it off," Mr. Boyle squints at Torey. "You do know that this isn't Home Economics, correct? That this is detention?"

Torey nods.

"Excellent," Boyle says with excitement, "We have enough for a game!"

Torey is disoriented. He assumed that he could just sit down and draw doodles on his book covers. He is not up for some kind of stupid game.

Boyle waves his hand for Simon to come on down off the bleachers and onto the gym floor.

Simon approaches with his usual demented grin. "What's up, Coach?"

Boyle tells him, "You two are captains. Killjoy picks first."

Killjoy, Kilroy, Torey hesitates. He doesn't know what is going on. He asks sheepishly, "What are we playing?"

Everyone including Boyle laughs menacingly. "We are going to enjoy a nice friendly game of Bombardment," says Boyle.

Torey stares blankly.

Rafael clarifies. "Dodgeball, dude."

Dodgeball! Dodgeball has been banned from California schools for decades, but its reputation for sheer reckless violence has kept it alive in realms of urban legend for all these years. Dodgeball is indeed banned from gym class, but this is detention making it exempt from such ridiculous rules, at least in Mr. Boyle's mind. Mr. Boyle is in the mindset that this sort of competition is just the thing to teach these miscreants about sportsmanship and becoming men.

Torey exhales nervously and considers his options. The last thing he needs is to face off with both twins. "I'll pick Sidney."

"Hey!" Simon barks, "You can't do that! You can't pick my brother."

Torey looks to Mr. Boyle to see if it is okay. Mr. Boyle tells Simon to, "Shut it, and pick."

"You are going down brah," Simon threatens.

Mr. Boyle steps between them. "Save your temper for the court, Pawling."

Simon checks his options, bulging muscle jock, thin wiry jock, or badass skateboard punk. Simon opts for size and hopefully roid rage. He picks Johnson.

Torey considers the remaining two, fully aware that his physical wellbeing is on the line. Howard or Rafael. It probably wouldn't matter either way. He tells Rafael, "Sorry, but these two are already set to beat each other up."

Rafael nods his head appreciating the logic. He tells Torey, "It's cool. I would have picked the same."

Mr. Boyle says enthusiastically, "Okay so it's Killjoy, Sidney, and Howard verses Simon, Johnson and Rafael." He has the boys line up facing the wall of folded wooden bleachers, each holding a red rubber ball.

"Your warm-up will consist of three throws against the wall. Starting now."

The six boys windup and throw the balls with all their might.

BAM! BAM! BAM! BAM! BAM! Bloop.

Five boys snicker. One blushes.

"Were you ready, Killjoy?" Boyle asks.

Torey chases down his ball that he threw, and makes a lame excuse. "I slipped."

His mind is spinning. *What the heck am I going to do? They're going to kill me. This is really going to hurt.* His panic is about to go nuclear when he remembers what his dad told him about the dynamics of delivering a blow. *Maybe if I try the same technique as throwing a punch*, he thinks.

Torey lines up with the other boys again for another volley against the bleachers. This time he puts his dad's techniques to use. He sets his stance. He maximizes his power with a twist of his hips as he steps forward. He follows through with his entire torso.

They throw. BAM! BAM! BAM! BAM! BAM! *BAM!*

Torey's throw was way off mark, but the explosive sound of rubber hitting wood is very satisfying. He was not expecting the ball to curve uncontrollably like it did. If only he could control it. He chases after his ball and remembers what Donovan told him about confidence and using his mind. Maybe he can guide it with his mind? He decides that no matter how painful this experience proves to be, he is going to work on nothing but throwing this stupid ball.

Torey lines up for his third and last throw. He is next to Johnson, but he takes a few steps away from him to give himself more room. This time he winds up and throws at an angle so that when the ball curves...BAM! BAM! BAM! BAM! BAM! *BAM!*

It hits its mark.

"Yes!" Mr. Boyle shouts, "We got us a game!" He is clearly unable to control his enthusiasm for the prospect of watching two teams full of testosterone and teen angst play out in a game of unrestrained violence.

As both teams take their sides, Torey wonders if he should ask about the rules, but it is too late; Mr. Boyle blows his whistle to start the game. Everyone immediately assumes a defensive posture holding the balls in front of their chests. They all look for an easy target.

Torey quickly rears back his ball, thinking that the implied threat will make the others think twice about throwing their balls at him. Unfortunately, this tactic leaves his body completely unprotected and makes him the easy target.

All three boys on Simon's team immediately launch their balls.

Torey barely manages to duck Rafael's throw, but Simon's ball slams into his ball knocking it out of his hands. Howard's throw nails him in the chest and knocks him to the floor.

Torey staggers to his feet and walks off the court to where Mr. Boyle stands, rubbing the spot where a welt is sure to form. "I never played this before," Torey explains.

"Watch and learn, kid."

Torey watches the rest of the game play out, taking note of the more experienced boys' tactics of defense and offense, as well as their gleeful expressions when nailing their opponents.

The game ends with Howard being the last man standing, meaning Torey's team lost. Mr. Boyle tells Torey, "This game is remarkable for its simplicity. Not too many rules. Hit your adversary with a ball, or catch his ball to get him out. Most importantly, avoid getting hit. Got it?"

"I think so. I'll do better next time," Torey promises.

"Next time is now, Killjoy. I got you boys 'til lunchtime."

The next two hours are a painfully long learning experience for Torey. For once in his life he is not worried about being cool or being uncool. He is only concerned with surviving.

"This will be the last game of the day," Mr. Boyle finally announces.

*I might actually get through this*, Torey thinks hopefully.

The game starts with a whistle and both teams square off. Torey has improved quickly, but has yet to get somebody out.

Instead of throwing every ball at Simon, he changes tactics and hauls one at Howard. A hard throw fueled by nearly two hours of pain and frustration. Howard puts his ball up for a block, but he underestimates Torey and his ball is blasted out of his hands and into his face. Both balls fall back to the gym floor.

Torey's first kill!

Torey finally gets to experience the feeling of jubilation and personal satisfaction that only a sport like dodgeball can offer, but his elation is short lived. Because of his years of being a bully magnet, he becomes concerned that Howard might decide to take it out on him.

Torey watches as Howard pulls at his nose with his thumb and forefinger, but as an athlete, Howard is a good sport. He offers Torey an appreciative nod for a good throw as he makes his way off the court. Johnson congratulates Torey with a fist bump.

Torey is surprised to realize that he might actually be starting to like this game. Sidney refuses to acknowledge Torey's score.

"Lets finish this," he announces to no one in particular.

The game resumes with a sudden flurry of throws. Rafael takes out Sidney with a shot to his knee. Johnson nails one off Rafael's shoulder only to be immediately hit by a ball thrown by Simon.

Two men left. Torey and Simon face off.

They throw simultaneously, each missing the other. While Simon's throw bounced straight back to Torey off the back wall, Simon has to chase after Torey's strange curveball. Simon attempts to keep one eye on Torey and locate the ball at the same time, but eventually he has to glance down.

Torey times it right and throws as hard as he can. Simon finally grabs a ball and looks up just in time for a facial. Torey's ball slams his cheek with a glorious *slap*.

Mr. Boyle blows his whistle. Game over.

"Yes!" Torey pumps his fists in the air thoroughly enjoying the greatest victory of his young life. He turns to smile at his teammates when suddenly a ball from off court smashes squarely into his face. He goes down hard and hits the floor with a thud.

A loud ringing in his ears prevents him from hearing Mr. Boyle balling out Sidney for being a low-life degenerate.

Torey regains his bearings despite the throbbing sting. He is less shocked from the pain than by the fact that he is actually able to take it.

Rafael extends a hand to help pull Torey to his feet. "You okay, dude?"

"I think so," Torey shakes his head and rolls his shoulders to shake off the sting. "What happened?"

"Your psycho teammate nailed you with a cheap shot."

Torey plays out his options in his mind: he could complain to Mr. Boyle to give Sidney detention from detention; he could throw his own cheap shot at his psycho teammate's head; or he can let it go and not give Sidney the satisfaction of getting a reaction.

Sidney is eagerly watching to see how this will play out. He is ready for a fight.

Torey takes a deep breath and decides to let this one go. He accepts Rafael's extended hand to be helped back up onto his feet. "Good playing."

"Not so bad yourself, Torey." They bump fists. Johnson and Howard each bump fists with Torey as they head out as well.

It has been quite a while since Torey has been called by his actual name by a classmate. His face blushes red with a warm feeling, or is that a welt that is forming from Sidney's ambush?

"Hey Kilroy," Mr. Boyle calls out, "I probably should not say this, but you are welcome back to detention anytime."

Torey smiles and waves at Mr. Boyle as he heads out of The Little Gym and back to his regularly scheduled classes.

Three hours later, Torey's ears are still ringing when the bell rings to signal the end of the school day. His bruised body is achy, but if you were to ask Torey how he felt, his answer would be, "Awesome, dude."

## Chapter 5

# *Wanna See Something Really Cool?*

Torey hits the beach as soon as possible. He appreciates how it sure does feel good to be back in the water. What a day. He paddles out to hang with Donovan and to tell him about one of the strangest days of his life.

Donovan waits impatiently. He is seething with aggravation that Torey did not show up this morning. *Doesn't this punk realize who he is dealing with? That time is short and I don't have a lot of time to set things straight?*

The ocean is choppy as if reflecting Donavan's sour mood, but it quickly settles down as Torey paddles closer and Donovan notices some of the nasty bruises and red marks that have yet to fade from Torey's torso. Donovan's jaw drops. He is suddenly concerned.

"Is everything okay, Kid?"

Torey is in an uncharacteristically calm state of mind. He simply smiles and nods.

Donovan says, "I must have missed you this morning."

"Oh sorry. My old man decided to teach me some fighting moves and wouldn't take no for an answer."

"Your Old Man did that to you?"

"What?" Torey realizes that Donovan must think that his father gave him the welts. "My father didn't hurt me. I got smacked up during dodgeball."

Donovan's facial expression reads as a question mark; he doesn't know dodgeball. Torey picks up on this and says, "Mr. Boyle called it Bombardment."

"Bombardment! I used to love bombardment," he says, remembering the good old days. The days before he got mixed up with a stinking mermaid. "It looks like you caught a beating."

Torey laughs. "I guess it took me a while to get the hang of it. He goes on to recount the rollercoaster ride of the day's events, the ups, the downs, getting sent to detention, choosing teams, the whole enchilada. He finishes with the account of Sidney blindsiding him with a shot to the face.

Donovan has to admit, "That sure is some day, kiddo." He sorts it out in his mind, considers every aspect, and every implication. He starts with, "Your old man can really fight?"

"He was a Navy Seal once."

"Okay, stick with that. He can teach you to fight like I cannot. I, on the other hand, will teach you how to develop your dynamism. With these two talents you could become the perfect storm."

"Dynamism?"

"How do you think I create my waves? How can I demonstrate this?" He considers for a moment as soft, billowy clouds gather on the horizon ready to set the scene for a perfect California sunset. Donovan grins. "Hey kid, you want to put a cherry on the top of this day?"

Torey was about to ask more about dynamism, but... "What do you mean?"

Donovan slides from his board and into the water. "Come on, I want to show you something."

Torey stays planted safely on his board and eyes him suspiciously.

Donovan slowly spins in a counter-clockwise motion with his arms outstretched. He quickly picks up speed until the area of water around him starts to resemble water funneling down a bath drain. Donovan allows himself to be sucked down.

Torey does not even consider getting off his board. He paddles back and away from the ever-expanding vortex.

Donovan's head breaks the surface a few feet away from the little whirlpool. He seems to give it more energy by making circular gestures with his hand and finger.

"Pretty cool right? You may have already guessed that when it comes to dynamism, water is my major element. My secondary element is air." Air corkscrews its way into the whirlpool and spirals downward.

"*That* is a pretty cool trick."

"It is more than just a trick, kid; this is your air supply."

Torey does not like the sound of this. "What are you talking about?"

"Why are you still sitting atop your board?"

Torey knows by the look on Donovan's face that he should get his butt in the water. It goes against his common sense, but he gives up the safety of his board and slips into the water next to the spinning vortex.

Donovan instructs him. "All I need you to do is keep your

head in the air funnel. You will be able to swim down far enough to see what's down there."

"What's down where?" Torey is quickly losing his sense of calmness. "How deep did you say we are going?"

"I don't want to spoil the surprise. Don't you trust me?" He doesn't wait for an answer as he sinks below the surface.

Torey reluctantly sucks in a breath and follows him, keeping his head in the air funnel. He is ten feet down before he remembers that he does not need to hold his breath; he forces himself to exhale and to try to breathe normally. He takes this moment to get accustomed to his surroundings. His vision through the submerged air is shimmery and distorted, but there is nothing to see anyway besides murky green fading to blackness. Donovan guides him down another twenty feet before swimming out of sight.

*This is not cool.*

Being alone this deep in the dark water causes Torey to panic. He looks frantically in all directions; all he can see is blurry darkness. He yells out, "Donovan," then he kicks his feet frantically to go back up to his board.

From somewhere, Donovan's voice, as if it were in his head, says, "Don't freak out on me now, kid."

Torey forces himself to not freak out, but he also does not relax. *How is he talking inside of my head?*

"I wasn't sure if it would work, but when we are both in the water we can communicate like this."

A sudden shimmery flash of movement in the distance catches Torey's attention. It must be some kind of big fish. *Maybe an Albacore,* he reasons. He strains his eyes to see it again.

A large shape flashes past going the other direction, but closer this time. He catches glimpses of other shadowy forms flitting by in all directions like sharks circling a wounded seal. A light glow of green phosphorescence trails after them as they pass. Torey becomes more and more alarmed.

*Sharks!*

He twists his head in all directions to try to keep track of them all. He does not want to be taken by surprise when they attack.

One of them swims straight at him. As it slowly glides out from the darkness, its form becomes less blurry until he can finally focus on what appears to be..."Oh my God, it's a freaking mermaid."

"Shh, you'll spook her," Donovan's voice warns playfully,

The mermaid circles him, showing off her exquisite form. She wears not a stitch of clothing, not even a bra made of seashells or starfish, and every movement of her lithe body strikes a chord in Torey's teenage hormone factory.

In the waning light, Torey can tell that her dark hair is red because of the highlights that flicker through it like embers from a fire. Torey is mesmerized, and hopes she comes closer so that he can see her face.

As if reading his mind, she darts right at him and stops just outside of the air funnel. Torey gasps audibly as her long billowy hair floats back off her face to reveal her magnificent beauty.

No makeup ever made could hope to improve on such a ravishing face. A face that is as soft and as flawless as a spring blossom. Her lips are plump and pouty. Delicate green scales glisten on her high cheekbones give a stunning effervescence to her appearance. But it is her eyes, her mesmerizing eyes, which demand full attention. The mermaid regards Torey with the saddest green eyes he has ever seen.

He could almost swear that she is crying, but they are under water so...

She smiles sadly at him and he knows that she must be the most beautiful girl he has ever seen. With all his being he wants to protect her, to care for her, to be with her. His heart pounds frantically. He feels that he is deeply in love with her.

She presses her face up to the vortex and into the funnel of air until they are nose-to-nose. She says something, but Torey cannot understand her. To him, her voice sounds like helium burps.

The incredible creature leans in closer to him and parts her sensuous lips; they look warm and pink and inviting. Torey realizes that his first kiss will be with a mermaid. His lips pucker like they have a will of their own. He thinks that he is supposed to close his eyes, but he couldn't shut them if he tried. He -

"Whoa!"

Donovan yanks the mermaid forcefully out of the air funnel. He spanks her tail and sends her darting off. He grabs Torey under the armpit to race him back to the surface.

Torey does not want to go back up. He pushes Donovan away and tries desperately to swim back down to be with the love of his life. Donovan hauls him up by an ankle. They resurface just in time for a most awesome sunset, but Torey does not care about it.

"Why did you pull me away from her?"

But all of Torey's thoughts of love, and longing, and forever after are fading. Torey grabs onto his board and floats for a while without speaking. He tries to wrap his mind around what just happened and if he really saw what he thinks he saw.

The sun extinguishes itself below the horizon; you could practically hear the sizzling hiss as it sinks into the water.

Donovan asks, "So tell me, are you still feeling lovey dovey?"

Torey laughs from nerves. "I actually feel a little freaked out now. Was that for real? That was so freaking intense."

"You just learned the lesson that I wish every day of my miserable life someone would have taught me: never kiss a stinking mermaid. They mess with you that way. Lying, deceitful, stunning sirens that they are."

"Oh, and by the way," he continues, "if your first kiss with a mermaid is while you are underwater, you will be as good as married to her, and you will dwell with her in the sea for the rest of your days. If you kiss a mermaid above the water, you will still be bound to her, but her tail will transform into legs and she will live with you on land until the day that you die. So I would recommend that you play it safe, and don't be kissing any stinking mermaids."

"Well then," Torey says, "thank you for dragging my dumb ass back up here." *That was close.* "Why can't she speak?"

"You heard her speak."

"But..."

"Mermaids only speak mermaid until they bond with a human. Once they bond, they will know and speak their mate's language."

"For the rest of your life? What happens to her after you die?"

"She will not have physically aged a single day. She will return to the sea until she can beguile another unfortunate soul."

"But this one was a teenager, right?"

"More like four or five hundred years old, at least."

Torey's mind is officially blown away and he has a million more questions. But they won't be answered, at least not right now.

"Sweet dreams, kid," Donovan says. He and his board dip below the surface to sink back down to the inky depths where the mermaids live.

\* \* \*

Torey slams through the kitchen door. He is amped out of his mind and he has to tell someone what happened, what he just saw, before like, before his head explodes.

His father sits at the kitchen table in front of an empty plate, across from Torey's full plate of now cold pork chops and applesauce. "You can nuke it after you visit your mom," he says. "She's been asking for you."

"Is she feeling better?" he asks?

Torey realizes that now is not a good time to bring up mermaids. Besides, *dad would probably kick my butt if I told him something so ridiculous.*

His dad doesn't bother to answer, so Torey heads off to her bedroom.

His mom has been pretty sick lately, but it comes and goes, kind of like June Gloom. Torey knocks on his Mom's door and peeks his head in. "Ma?"

"Come in darling," she responds. The room is lit only from the light of the moon that glows through the open window. A cool breeze rustles the curtains. She squints when he flicks on the light.

Mrs. Leona Kilroy is pale from her illness. *Pale as a goth,* Torey thinks.

Despite being ill, his mom is still one good-looking woman. She sports a short Betty Paige-styled hair doo straight out of the fifties. She turns heads for sure; the Beachcomber has definitely married up.

Torey has only known his mom to be a figure of health. He doesn't remember seeing her sick a day in her life. He is uncertain as to how to handle this situation.

"You're looking better," he lies.

"I'm feeling better," she lies. "I am sure that it's just an allergy, the Santa Anna winds or something. She changes the subject. "You seem to grow another inch everyday."

Torey didn't realize it until now that he has been going through a growth spurt. If he ever wore long pants, he would certainly have noticed that they would all be high waters on him now.

"How is school?"

"School? School is interesting." He doesn't know what else to say; the last thing he wants to do is to tell her about wedgies. Or dodgeball. Or detention.

"What do you mean 'interesting'?" she pushes.

He changes the subject. "Dad is teaching me how to fight. How to defend myself."

She seems surprised at this. "Well, just try not to get your hopes up; your dad was never much of a fighter."

Torey is becoming used to his mom's odd moments, but what the heck is she talking about? "He was a Navy Seal. Of course he can fight."

Leona seems disoriented. She begins to zone out. She exhales sharply.

"It's just that...well, okay, and I will admit that it might be all in my head, but things don't feel right. My memories are...my memories aren't always the way that I remembered them."

"Ma! You're freaking me out!"

Leona snaps out of it, stunned by her son's outburst. She grasps the fact that Torey is entering the "leaving the nest" phase that all teens go through whether they know it or not. She makes a decision that no matter how she feels tomorrow, she will force herself to get out of bed and be the mother that Torey needs.

"I will be up and about by tomorrow. I promise."

Torey hugs her, "You better, because Dad is going to kill me with his cooking."

## Chapter 6

# *How To Not Be A Bully Magnet*

Saturday morning, the morning after the strangest day of his life, Torey wolfs down a plate of last night's leftovers, cold and very not tasty. Some time between chewing his last bite and stepping outside, he decides not to tell his father about yesterday's detention, dodgeball, and especially not about mermaids.

His father greets him with, "Did you do your pushups?"

"Fifty pushups and fifty sit ups," Torey answers.

The training begins with more exercises. Not jumping jacks and such, but hardcore drills that are designed to build core strength and striking power. After twenty minutes, Torey feels it in every muscle; a dull pain that he is surprised to admit feels more good than bad.

"Okay, so that move I showed you yesterday will only get you so far. Today you will learn a follow up move and then a second follow up move. That should get you through your first fight."

First fight! Torey's habitual fight or flight emotions well up in his head. Insecurity still rules his young mind. He momentarily shrinks from the thought of it. He hopes that his dad didn't notice his lack of confidence.

The next hour is spent repeating the elbow-uppercut-to-the triceps move followed by a knee-to-the-gut move and ending with a strike to the face. Each time the Beachcomber mixes it up with a different move of his own. He sometimes reacts offensively, sometimes defensively, teaching Torey to adapt to different possible scenarios.

"Isn't this a bit rough for a schoolyard fight?" Torey asks.

"Schoolyard fight? I am teaching you how to fight criminals, psychos and enemy combatants," his father informs him.

"Enemy combatants? Are you for real?"

His father gets serious. "What I'm saying is, I am training you to take on a worst case scenario. I am not telling you to take out a school kid. Just use what you need to end the fight, and end it as soon as possible. If one move at half strength is enough to stop your opponent, leave it at that, that's cool. But if your life is in danger, you should be prepared to take the chooch down."

Torey repeats the word, "Chooch."

They round off for one more go. Torey is getting to feel the flow of it. He has enough confidence to try something a little different this time.

He attacks lefty. The old man is taken off guard; he actually back-peddles a couple of steps. One strike grazes the razor stubble on his chin. Torey pulls back suddenly and puts his hands up to signal a break.

The Beachcomber is surprised, but relieved that he didn't have to use a move that might have shaken Torey's newfound confidence. He rethinks his initial reaction and admits to himself that he actually feels a sense of pride for his son. "What's up?"

"Is Mom on medication?" Torey asks. "She is acting weird."

The Beachcomber sighs and walks over to the bench next to the second-hand picnic table. "She is definitely not on medication, but yeah I'm a little concerned as well. I have never seen her this bad, and you know that she will never go to a doctor. She prefers her own remedies."

"What's up with that?" asks Torey.

"Have you ever seen a doctor?" his father asks him.

The thought had never crossed Torey's mind until now. "No. When I was born I guess."

The Beachcomber shakes his head and grins remembering, "She gave birth to you in the bathtub. No doctors present. She doesn't believe in them."

"Holy crap." He considers the potential danger that his infant self was in all those many years ago. "So what are we going to do to get her healthy?"

Before the Beachcomber can respond the door flies open.

His mom strides out, vibrant and flush with energy. A far cry from how she looked yesterday.

She practically sings. "And how are my strapping young men this morning?"

She carries a tray that is teeming with a breakfast of pancakes, scrambled eggs, sliced pineapple, and orange juice. She sets it on the picnic table.

Torey grabs her in a bear hug and spins her around. "Mom, you're back!"

Leona is also surprised. "When did you get so big and strong?

It's a good thing that I cooked up a man's breakfast for you."

Torey and his parents sit down for breakfast and enjoy a rare moment of normalcy.

* * *

After breakfast, Torey is back on his board paddling out to meet Donovan. The Pacific gets chilly this time of year, but it does not bother Torey; he is used to being cold as he grew up in a beach house with no heat except for a fireplace in the living room. He has spent many cold nights under a thin blanket.

Torey is intently scanning the water trying to spot a mermaid when Donovan breaks surface next to him. Torey hardly flinches. "Are they here?"

Donovan shakes his head. "I don't think so. You know, when we first completed the portal, I figured that they would swim off and never come back, but they always return. I just cannot figure mermaids out."

"Why don't you just ask them?"

"I don't speak mermaid."

"That's right. You would have to bond with one first, right?"

Donovan nods. "And I learned my lesson about bonding with mermaids."

They float quietly for a few moments. Donovan is the first to break the silence. "So what did you notice about the cool kids at school?"

Torey is disappointed. He wants to talk more about mermaids. "Cool kids don't care about anything."

Donovan shakes his head. "On the surface you are partially right. Cool kids don't let on that things bother them, but they actually care about quite a lot. They care about sports, their cars, and their families, whatever. What they do not care about is what you or anyone else thinks or says about them." He splashes a spray of water at Torey to make sure he is paying attention.

"Call it what you will — water off a duck's back, or being thick-skinned."

Torey thinks it over. "Okay, that makes sense, I think. But when do I become cool?"

"You are already well on your way to being cool. For the first time in your life you got sent to detention and you handled it in a way that let people know that it didn't bother you. You played dodgeball and actually enjoyed it. And you let people know that you can take a hit like a man."

"I didn't even realize that I was already becoming cool," Torey says.

"Now, don't be getting ahead of yourself, James Dean. You still need to turn the tables on your tormentors. You will need to humiliate them and you need to humiliate them publically."

Torey pauses. "Sidney and Simon?"

"Yes, Sidney and Simon are blocking your progress. They are also blocking your dynamism. You need to remove that blockage like Roto-rooter if you are ever going to be cool."

"You're not serious. You mean I can really learn dynamism?"

Donovan explains. "I admit that I went off on a tangent with that and you are probably not ready for it, but..." He gives Torey the once over and then continues. "Everything is ruled by energy. The world would not exist without it. Dynamism is the control over energy. It is historically a Pagan practice, but it is really a natural phenomenon that any living being can use. But to use it you must be aware of it."

Torey cannot believe what he just heard, "So you really can

teach me how to make waves with magic?"

Donovan puts out both hands to motion for Torey to calm the heck down. Torey settles, but only a little. Donovan corrects his use of the word magic. "Dynamism. Yes, you have seen me use it."

Torey is so excited he cuts Donovan off, "Like when you brought me down to see mermaids."

"Control of air is my secondary dynamism. Water is my primary. I have no power over earth or fire." Donovan stops talking; he notices another questioning look on Torey's face.

Torey puts two and two together. "Water and Air," he says. "So it is you who is creating this weird June Gloom."

Donovan grins sheepishly, knowing full well that he has been caught with his hand in the pickle barrel. "You didn't really think that was natural did you?"

"But, why?"

"Because I cannot afford to be noticed. Not until I bag me my treacherous mermaid. Besides, I can't be seen out here creating waves and teaching you how to wield magic..."

"Dynamism," Torey corrects him.

Donovan continues. "And how to be cool."

It makes sense. Torey's head is still spinning, but he seems to have better control of his enthusiasm. *This is intense.*

"So when do we start?"

"We have already started," answers Donovan. "I am assuming that your infatuation with the ocean is an indication that water is your primary dynamism. I mean, you would rather be here than anywhere else. Do you have a noticeable inclination to air, earth or fire?"

Torey thinks. "Well, I definitely like to breathe. I like to walk, too. I'm not a pyro like that kid Ronald in sixth grade, so it's probably not fire."

He looks eagerly to Donovan. "Does that help?"

"No, that does not help at all." Donovan's mood swings suddenly from cool and calm to grouchy and impatient. The water around them turns choppy. Torey knows enough to shut up and wait for Donovan's mood swing to pass. And it does.

Donovan exhales sharply. "We will start with water. Now don't go over-thinking it or trying too hard, but just imagine that you can already do it, imagine that you have been doing it for years. Create a current to move your surfboard."

Torey scrunches his forehead as he tries to will the water to do his bidding.

"Stop scrunching your head."

"But-"

"It's like breathing. You don't wrinkle your forehead when you inhale, do you?"

*How can it be that easy?* Torey takes a deep breath.

Donovan can see Torey's frustration. This is something that Torey has to wrap his mind around. Donovan is short on patience and decides that Torey might benefit from a little encouragement. He watches as Torey looks at the water, and then uses his own dynamism to give Torey's board a little shove.

"Whoa! What was that? Did I do that? I like, totally felt my board move!"

Donovan encourages him. "Not too smooth, but you did it. It will get easier with practice.

"I can't believe this stuff is for real."

Donovan will have to wait and see if his little deception will be of any help, but now something has caught his attention. "They are on the beach this very moment."

"Who is on the beach?"

"Your bully twins."

Torey wants to ask how he can see all of this through the fog, but before he can, Donovan says, "Here's the plan, kid. You cruise up to the shoreline and step off your board like you own the place. It's time to confront your nemesis, but be sure to stay in the water where I can trip them up if needed."

"This is too soon. I'm not ready."

Donovan continues. "They will come to you. You will not respond to their taunts. You will play it cool and you will keep your mouth shut. Not one word. Do you hear me? You will focus on the task at hand. Are you following me?"

"But–"

Donovan presses on. "They aren't expecting you to fight back, let alone use the moves your old man taught you. But if the element of surprise is not enough, or if you falter, I will use my dynamism over water to trip them up and keep them off balance."

"That doesn't seem fair," Torey says innocently.

"This is not about being fair," Donovan insists. "Is two older ruffians fighting against one kid being fair? This is about letting them know that you are no longer an easy mark. Once we have restored balance, you can worry about playing fair."

Torey fidgets uneasily on his board as he stresses over what is about to go down with the Appalling Twins. His subconscious mind is shifting back and forth from flight to fight.

Donovan understands that this kid is still, in his mind, a kid. What the boy needs is a firm push. He knows that he must not set Torey's expectations too high; Torey cannot be disappointed in the end.

"For now, it is more important to make an impression than to actually win a fight. It is more important to just face them like a man and get in one good shot. Do this and you will never again have to suffer another wedgie."

"Okay," Torey says.

Donovan uses his dynamism to glide the board forward. Torey stands up and rides it towards the shoreline. He looks back, hoping that Donovan will change his mind. A three-foot wave forms and Torey rides it towards the shoreline.

Torey's mind is freaking out in a big way. *Why is Donovan pushing me to do this so soon?*

But a strange thing happens in Torey's mind on his way to his first fight. He starts to intersperse his thoughts of panic with calmly recounting a mental checklist of the moves his father has taught him. He then decides which moves he will start with.

*This is going to happen, and I am going to get in at least one good shot.*

* * *

Sidney and Simon have spent the morning scouring the beach looking for Torey; they are not at all happy with how things played out in dodgeball, but their attention spans are short.

"People always tell me I got no common sense, but I don't even know what common sense is," Simon tells Sidney.

"That's because you're a dumb ass."

"What, like you have common sense?"

"Pop always tells me I got the sense of a bag of nails," Sidney says, "so at least I got sense. You don't even got no common sense."

Simon takes offense and pushes his brother which escalates

into the two of them grappling for headlocks.

One of the six teens that were getting ready to play volleyball notices the commotion and points it out to his friends. They all rush over to see what is going on.

\* \* \*

Torey rides his wave to shore. He can't help but notice the twins are rolling in the sand wrestling each other, and he hopes that they tire each other out.

Sidney adjusts his headlock and grinds Simon's head into the wet sand. From his new vantage point, Simon can see Torey riding a wave and is heading right for them. He punches his brother's side for attention and chokes out, "Tool...Tool...Tool."

"Don't call me that!" Sidney yells.

Simon manages to point a finger until Sidney finally spots Torey. He grins and releases his brother's head. Sidney cracks all of his knuckles by rolling his two fists together in anticipation of delivering a beating.

Simon gets up and shakes the sand from his hair. He yells at Torey. "Hey tool, get off our wave!"

Torey rushes them as soon as the fin scrapes the sand. He pushes Sidney hard into Simon, but instead of pressing forward like his father taught him, he waits to see what the twins will do next.

The crowd of kids is stunned. *Is that Torey kid trying to commit suicide?*

Donovan's head bobs unseen in the water at the edge of the fog. His eyes are as wild as those of the kids on the beach.

The twins trade evil grins and rush at Torey.

Torey moves to sidestep the twins just as a surge of water

crashes against the three of them. The water causes Simon to lose his balance and he trips over Torey's out-stretched leg. Sidney manages to keep his stance and goes after Torey, but Torey keeps just out of Sidney's reach by keeping the fallen Simon between them.

Simon finally stops flailing in the water and regains his footing. Out of sheer frustration, Sidney pushes his brother into Torey. Torey sidesteps to the right, blocks Simon's off balance punch, and with a hip twist to add strength to his blow, he strikes his fist into Simon's stomach. Simon gasps and clutches his gut, splashing back down into Donovan's turbulent water, but still trying to grab at Torey's ankles.

Torey does exactly what Donovan told him not to do; he steps up onto the dry sand and squares off with Sidney like his father taught him. Sidney charges Torey and plows into him with all his weight. His shoulder hits hard into Torey's left bicep, but Torey manages to shift his stance. He lands a solid punch on Sidney's face and then uses his momentum to throw him down.

Torey looks to Simon who is still flailing about where Donovan is tripping him up with strong currents of water. Torey decides to do something both reckless and symbolic. He charges the off-balance Simon and pulls him out of the water by the band of his shorts and bum rushes him up to the dry sand, wedgie-style. He shoves him down next to his brother for a sandy coating of shake-n-bake right in front of the crowd of his awe- struck peers.

Sidney has never been punched before, except by his brother. It hurts his pride more than it does his face. "What the hell is wrong with you?" he yells at Torey.

Torey stands his ground. He knows that if he tried to talk his voice would crack, or fail him altogether.

The six kids who witnessed the event are stunned. They don't know whether to cheer for Torey or...or...

They stare silently, mouths agape. Nothing makes sense anymore. It's like hell just froze over. Torey freaking Kilroy is a badass!

The twins are more confused than actually hurt, though Sidney still rubs the spot on his face where Torey hit him. They are not inclined to continue fighting.

Torey is as confused as everyone else. His face goes pale as his adrenaline slams to a halt. A flood of emotions overwhelms him; he couldn't celebrate if he tried. He does the only thing he can think of: he turns his back to the crowd, dives onto his board, and paddles like a western movie hero into the sunset (or in this case, into the fog).

Torey does not realize it, but at that moment, his cool rating, as perceived through the eyes of his peers, has elevated tenfold.

Donovan is beside himself with glee. He waits for Torey to glide in before spilling it.

"Dude! I was concerned when you stepped out of the water, but damn, I gotta hand it to your old man, he taught you some serious moves."

Torey finally relaxes enough to laugh and release his emotions. "I feel so...so...I don't know how I feel, but I feel..."

Donovan offers the word, "Stoked?"

"I feel stoked."

"Get used to it, kid. You are officially no longer a bully magnet."

Donovan reaches out a hand, palm up, for high five. Torey smiles and stares down the hand.

"What, you don't want to high five?" Donovan asks.

Torey reaches out a fist. Donovan does the same. They celebrate with a fist bump.

"Hey kid?" Donovan says after a moment.

"Yeah?"

"It's almost time we catch that mermaid of mine."

"Yeah?"

"For now, just keep an eye out for a woman who stands apart from the rest. She will resemble a teenager, but will seem wise beyond her years. She will be at least as beautiful as the mermaid that you have already met."

"Will I fall in love with her too?"

"I would expect so. You might even have a crush on her already. She may even dwell in your school."

Torey's mind races to thoughts of Cassandra. *No, that would be crazy, right? I've never seen her in the water. I hope it isn't her.*

"School, right," he says. "I'll keep an eye out. I promise."

"I'll catch you later," Donovan says. "I have some skulls that need stacking."

With that, he sinks into the water, leaving Torey floating alone with his thoughts.

Torey doesn't always get Donovan's weird sense of humor, but for the first time in a long while, Torey cannot wait for the weekend to be over so that he can go to school. Maybe it will be different for him on Monday. He is not convinced that he is officially cool yet, but at least he is no longer exactly "uncool."

# Chapter 7

## *Beauty And The Least*

Torey steps outside and greets Monday morning with a smile and a newfound sense of confidence. *T.G.I.M baby.* His thoughts are interrupted when his dad comes at him with a sneak attack.

They spar back and forth trading strikes and defending counterattacks well into the morning. The Beachcomber gains the advantage by sweeping Torey's legs out from under him. Torey lands on his back, but is not ready to give up. He spins on his butt to face his attacking father. He pins his dad's ankles with his feet. His dad is caught by surprise and has no choice but to reach down for a fistful of Torey's shirt. Torey grabs the outstretched arm with one hand, pulls his father off balance, then throws a punch at his unprotected face. He grazes it slightly before his stunned father pins him. He is close, but no cigar. Not this time.

His dad extends a hand to help Torey.

"You are getting pretty cocky after winning your first fight. I never taught you that move. I will have to remember not to take you for granted any more."

Torey wonders if that is a backhanded compliment, but he is not used to being complimented by his father at all, so he will take it.

"Did you ever...take someone down, or out, or...?" Torey's voice trails off.

"Are you trying to ask if I ever killed somebody?" his father asks. "War is hell, and there is only one way to survive it, and that is a discussion for another day."

He grabs a towel to dry off and heads back into the house.

Torey considers his dad's words as he heads to the bus stop. Everyone thinks Jasper Kilroy is just a weird beachcomber and a loser. Torey always assumed they were right, but now he considers. *Maybe my dad is a war hero and maybe I'm not the son of a loser, and maybe everyone should keep their stupid opinions to themselves.*

He is so lost in his thoughts that he hardly realizes that the school bus is already down the street and he just missed it. Just a week ago he would have moped, went back home, and asked for a ride to school. But this week things have changed. Torey has definitely changed. Everything is different. Without a second thought he jogs the two miles to school.

* * *

School is abuzz with talk of Torey's fight with the twins. It is even dubbed "The Appalling Beat Down. Those who witnessed the event recount every detail to those who weren't there." Those who weren't there refuse to believe it, but in years to come, everyone will claim to have been there.

Most are just excited that somebody finally put the twins in their place. Frustration sets in when it becomes obvious that the twins have not yet shown up for school, and probably won't. And that Torey was not on the bus.

Torey is still a couple blocks away when he hears the school bell ring. When he finally arrives, there is no one in the hall as he makes his way to homeroom.

All heads turn eagerly, including Cassandra's, as he strides through the homeroom door.

"You are late, Mr. Kilroy," says Mr. Nussman expectantly.

Torey shrugs. He confidently smiles and makes eye contact with Cassandra before he takes his seat behind her. Mr. Nussman's aggravation is apparent as he tries to quiet the excited whispers of his students.

"You seem to be a real distraction today, Mr. Kilroy. Are you fishing for another day of detention?"

Torey smiles confidently. "It's all cool, Mr. Nussman."

Mr. Nussman's eyes go wide, but he decides to drop it and goes back to taking attendance.

Despite his outward show of bravado, Torey is a bundle of nerves. He must push from his mind his past disastrous attempts to speak to girls. He stares at the back of Cassandra's head and takes a deep breath in order to steady himself.

Cassandra is as surprised by his behavior as is the rest of the class and wants to get a good look at this new Torey. She would have to turn completely around, but is reluctant to do so.

Torey whispers to the back of her head. "Hi Cassandra."

Cassandra is thankful for an excuse to turn around. "You sure gave everybody something to talk about."

"Do you want to go with me to the Shake Shack after school?" Torey blurts out. He has never asked a girl out before and is not aware of the correct protocol.

Cassandra's pale makeup is not enough to hide the blushing of her cheeks.

The entire class cannot believe that Torey, the nerd-wannabe-surfer-boy, just asked out Cassandra, the Queen of Darkness, in front of the entire class. She manages to keep her cool.

"My, but aren't you just full of surprises these days."

"We can sit under an umbrella out of the sun, and I would really like to ask your opinion, well, your *advice* about something."

Cassandra is relieved that Torey slightly pulled it back from being an official date. Her mind races. *What is he thinking? Doesn't he realize that I have a reputation to uphold?*

She can feel the stares of everyone waiting for her answer. She is all about shock value, and decides to blow their minds. She grins. Loudly enough for everybody to hear, she says, "It's a date."

* * *

The Shake Shack is a popular sandwich and milkshake shop on the Pacific Coast Highway that sits on a cliff with an idyllic view of the ocean. It is a modest establishment with wooden picnic tables and benches for outside seating only. Every honest local will recommend the Monkey Flip, a milkshake made with bananas and peanut butter, but it is not on the menu. You have to be "in the know" to order it. It is late afternoon, and the Shack is crowded with surfers and teens.

Cassandra watches the scene from behind the tinted windows of her mom's white Lexus. Her mom, Leslie Covent, was once an aspiring soap opera actress until she got herself knocked up by the producer, now her husband. She still thinks that she could have been a big star, but is just as content to spend her days tanning poolside and spending her husband's money in posh Beverly Hills boutiques. She sports a perfect tan to accessorize her platinum blonde hair and strapless white sundress, unlike her ghostly daughter who directs her to, "Pull over here."

Mrs. Covent does as she is told, but responds with, "I just love your new dress. Is it the new shade of black that all the girls are talking about?"

Cassandra rolls her eyes as she flips down the visor to check her appearance and apply a fresh coat of nearly black lipstick. She runs her fingers through her pin straight, long black hair and flips up the visor.

Cassandra's mom is one of the few people who is aware of how beautiful her daughter is without any makeup, but as she watches her now, she can see how the pale makeup and dark eyeliner really does make her stand out. Yet she refuses to encourage her daughter's macabre sense of style.

"Cassie, for pity's sake! This is a first date. Try not to scare him off."

"It's not a date," Cassandra replies a little too quickly. "And my name is Cassandra."

Cassie…Cassandra looks out the window.

"Just look at this. It's a circus out there. I don't even know why I accepted his invitation, except to maybe freak out the troglodytes in homeroom. Maybe we should leave."

Her mom dabs her own lips with gloss and ignores the request to leave.

Cassandra continues. "I mean, look at this - there isn't even a wisp of shade left, what with those so-called sun worshippers glomming up all of the umbrellas."

Her mom pops open the glove box displaying an array of sunscreen sprays and lotions. "Be my guest."

"As if." Cassandra turns back to her view of the Shake Shack and spots Torey as he pulls a large umbrella from the hole in the center of the only empty table.

"There he is," Cassandra whispers.

She watches with wide eyes as he carries the large umbrella past the rest of the tables and towards the car. She can't help but notice that he changed his tee shirt for a button-down Hawaiian print shirt.

"Oh my God, is that him?" Cassandra's mom asks. "He is adorable. Is that tan for real? And look, he is bringing the shade to you."

Cassandra does not acknowledge her mom's comment. She did not know what she was expecting, but she was not expecting Torey to act so... so gallant.

"Mom, I need you to hang around okay? I need an excuse to cut this short and you're it."

Torey arrives at the car, plants the point of the umbrella into the grassy sand and knocks on Cassandra's window.

Cassandra opens the window. "Lets do this."

Mrs. Covent smiles and winks at Torey as her daughter swings open the door and steps out for her unlikely date. Torey holds the umbrella with both hands and angles it so that not a ray of sunlight has the opportunity to caress Cassandra's fair skin.

Cassandra can't help but be touched by this rather bold gesture from this somewhat peculiar boy. She places a hand on his bicep, partly to acknowledge his consideration, and partly to freak out those who came here only to gawk at her and Torey.

Torey replaces the umbrella back into the table. Cassandra takes a seat under the shade and waits for Torey to say something. He quickly catches a passing waitress.

"Hi, two Monkey Flips please." When she walks away, Torey notices the displeased look on Cassandra's face.

"I am perfectly capable of ordering for myself," she says.

"Oh, sorry. I can catch her before she places the order, but a Monkey Flip is the best that they got."

Cassandra can tell that Torey is nervous. She decides to give him a break.

"No, that's fine. I would have ordered my usual, but maybe it's time I try something new," she smiles.

"Your usual?" Torey asks.

"Seltzer water, no fruit."

Torey cannot relate to her usual drink and has no idea of how to respond to that. Before an awkward silence can set in Torey changes the subject.

"Don't get me wrong, but you believe in the supernatural right? Vampires and stuff?"

Cassandra is taken aback by this blunt and ridiculous question. "Are you for real?"

Torey explains. "A week ago, I would have been certain that vampires didn't exist, but now, after what I have seen, I am not so sure."

"I am a goth, not a vampire, but are you trying to tell me that you saw a vampire?"

Torey laughs nervously. "Well, not a vampire, but something equally unreal."

Cassandra waits for an explanation, but gets none. She finally says "I have never seen a vampire, so I can't say for sure whether they exist or not."

"Why did you become a goth?" Torey asks.

Cassandra isn't sure that she even knows the answer to that one.

"I always felt that I was different..."

This is a subject that she is not going to get into. She quickly changes the topic.

"Why do you sit in the water all day? Everyone knows there aren't waves anymore."

Torey knows that Cassandra has a point, but he cannot tell her about Donovan.

"I feel at home in the water. It is the only place where I feel like me. I never feel like me anywhere else - not at school, not at home...it's kind of hard to explain."

Cassandra doesn't need him to explain. She would never admit it to anyone, but once upon a time, she was an awkward, shy girl, at least until she went goth. Suddenly she was an unknown, a freak maybe, but not a geek. So much better than being treated like a geek.

But she is definitely not going to discuss something so personal on a first date.

*First date? This is not a date!* But she admits, if only to herself, that Torey has sparked her interest.

The waitress arrives and places two Monkeys Flips in front of them.

"Wait a minute," Cassandra says suddenly. "I've seen the drawings on your book covers! You're not going to tell me that you saw a mermaid, are you?"

The waitress looks at Torey as if she, too, is waiting for him to answer Cassandra's question. Torey's face blushes despite his California tan.

"Don't be silly," Torey says defensively.

*That was easy.* Torey wasn't sure how he was going to bring up the subject of mermaids, but Cassandra did it for him. He waits for the nosey waitress to leave. "Shh," and whispers. "Keep it down, will you?"

Cassandra looks Torey in the eye trying to decide if he is messing with her or not. She takes a sip of her Monkey Flip. She had almost forgotten how good calories taste. She smiles at Torey and suddenly realizes just how deep blue his eyes are.

*If she were a mermaid she wouldn't just blurt out the word mermaid, or would she?* Torey decides to change the subject. Of course she is not a mermaid, and he does not want her to think that he is a complete idiot. All he knows is that he has a serious crush on her and he does not want to blow it. But, she isn't ready to drop it.

"I saw a show about mermaids on the Nature Channel once. They looked kind of like monkey people with fish tails. Really freaky!"

Torey smiles and shakes his head. "Did you think that my drawing looked like a freaky sea monkey?

"Well no, but I didn't realize that was an actual portrait. Maybe it's a mermaid from Greek mythology. Those ones were supposed to be really beautiful."

Torey cannot tell if Cassandra is just humoring him and suddenly feels self conscious about even discussing this with her on their first date. He wants to change the subject.

"Maybe. Or maybe I just saw a big fish."

"You are a strange boy," Cassandra tells him, "but I will do some research on mermaids and see if we can figure out what it is that you saw."

She sees the disappointed look on his face. "Not that there is anything wrong with strange boys."

She takes his well-tanned hand, which strikes a distinct contrast in her pale grasp. "But I will tell you one thing, if I ever saw a vampire, I would run like hell."

They share a good laugh which helps break the tension.

Cassandra slurps the last of her monkey flip and declares, "This was fun, but I promised my mom that I would help her with something. We should do this again."

Torey doesn't want the date to end so soon.

"Are you sure that you want to leave before the sunset? We have a great view from here."

"Are you trying to get romantic Torey Kilroy?" Cassandra asks playfully. She is hoping to see him blush again and is not disappointed.

"We still have an audience," she reminds him.

He had completely forgotten about the kids from school who are pretending not to be looking and talking about them. He stands.

"Well, okay, but at least let me walk you back to the car."

She looks into his eyes and smiles.

"What?" he asks self-consciously.

"You," she replies coyly.

Torey reaches for the umbrella, but Cassandra stops his hand.

"A few rays won't kill me."

Torey takes this as being a good sign. He keeps hold of her hand and walks with her slowly back to her mom's car. As they approach, they are amused to notice her mom belting out a song along with the radio. It's an old sixties tune about miracles.

Cassandra is relieved that her mom is oblivious to their presence. She seizes the moment and plants a soft peck of a kiss on

Torey's cheek. Well, mostly his check. When her lips accidently brush the corner of his lips, they are both stunned by the rush of electricity that surges through them. She allows her lips to linger for longer than she intended, then quickly pulls away from Torey, feeling dazed. Cassandra's mom turns to look just a moment too late.

Cassandra is confused and out of sorts and disturbed by the sudden feeling of not being in control. She does not know what else to do but rush into the car and order her mom to, "Go. Just drive."

*What have I done? He better not get the idea that he's my boyfriend.*

Torey watches them drive off. He is oblivious to the whistles and comments called out by some of the juvenile patrons at the Shack. His head is spinning with a torrent of emotions.

He turns his back on the Shake Shack and begins his long trek home. Torey wants to rerun the entire first date through his mind, but all he can manage to think about is the kiss and this strange and overwhelming feeling of love for Cassandra.

# Chapter 8

## *Dynamism Shmynamism*

Torey wakes at 4 a.m. the next morning, full of energy and raring to go. Thoughts of his first kiss will not let him fall back asleep. Through his open window, he hears the sound of waves crashing, which has been a rarity lately. He climbs out of bed, gets dressed, and goes outside to check it out.

It is two hours before sunrise and still pitch black. A line of white foam defines the shoreline as a wave crashes against it.

Torey has always surfed a shortboard and had no interest in longboards- too old school. But Donovan has caused him to wonder what they are like. He heads for the rack of surfboards and selects a nine-foot longboard.

Torey heads off into the darkness without a second thought and wades into the inky water. He is so happy that there are waves again that he doesn't hesitate to test the new board on his first real wave in a long time. It's not a large wave by any means, but he is surprised by how long a ride he is able to milk from this board. His vision is limited so he relies on his sense of feel to maneuver the waves. He spends the next hour testing its limits. On wave after wave he steps further and further to the nose of the board. He thoroughly enjoys every success as well as every wipeout.

Torey takes a break and lays back on his board to check out something that he has never seen before- a false dawn. A false dawn is a bright pyramid of light that sometimes shines over the eastern horizon on dark moonless nights just before dawn. Poets and writers have referred to the false dawn as symbolizing a moment of false hope or false promise.

Torey tries gesturing his hands like Donovan did when he created the whirlpool, willing the water to swirl. It does, ever so slightly, but it swirls!

He redoubles his efforts. The water suddenly spins into a small vortex as the air is sucked nearly three inches into the ocean. Torey becomes distracted when he realizes that he doesn't feel the water sucking in the air.

He feels the air responding to his thoughts and pushing into the water. The small whirlpool collapses in on itself. Tiny air bubbles float back up to the surface. Torey laughs out loud, fully charged by his first small success.

*This stuff is really possible*, he thinks, *but it should be the water, not the air, responding to me.* He feels no control over the water that he feels totally at home in.

*Air must be my primary dynamism. Water is probably secondary. I guess that is okay. I will have to keep on practicing.*

The sun rises to shed light on Torey's new world.

Torey has worked up quite a hunger and he is now distracted by the thought of wolfing down a hearty breakfast. He takes one last look at the ocean in the light of dawn and catches one last wave all the way to the shore.

* * *

As Torey returns home, he immediately notices the new addition to the yard. He must have missed it in the dark, but an eight-foot Polynesian-looking Tiki pole has appeared next to the patio. It must weigh a ton, but somehow his dad managed to drag it home. He has dragged a lot of strange things home in the past, but never something as cool as this. It is almost three feet wide and features deep carvings of a Polynesian god or warrior or something. Torey runs his hand down its face to appreciate the feeling of its well-worn ornate carving. It has faded stains of old its old color, but it is mostly worn to the grey tones of driftwood.

He wonders how old this thing is and where it came from. He also cannot help but notice that there are four arrows grouped tightly in a knot of wood where its heart would be. This is weird even for his father.

Torey turns to go inside and is startled to see his dad sitting quietly at the picnic table. Mr. Kilroy is filthy and exhausted from digging the hole that the Tiki pole is set in. He strikes a wood match and lights a fat cigar. He drags the flame into the tube of tobacco and puffs out a smoke ring.

"How did you like the longboard?" he asks.

"It's good," Torey tells him. "It's an entirely different ride, but it's kind of fun." He asks, "Are those arrows?"

The beachcomber studies his boy, a boy that is quickly becoming a young man.

"I myself probably would not have tried a first ride on a longboard all alone in the dead of night. Those are crossbow bolts."

Torey kind of understands the old man's concern about

night surfing.

"I was awake and it's not like our television works anymore or anything. Crossbow bolts?"

His father gestures to the Tiki pole. "Have you ever seen one of these before?"

"Maybe in a magazine or a text book. Why?"

"Well let me know if you do. It's important."

"Yeah, sure," Torey answers. "Since when do you smoke cigars?"

His father half-scowls. "It's an old habit."

"And it's like, six o'clock in the morning," Torey adds.

The beachcomber wants to cut this line of questioning. "Your mom doesn't like it. She also doesn't like bacon, but there is a plate of it inside. You better hurry up and eat it before she wakes."

That is all Torey needs to hear. He rushes inside for the rare plate of bacon.

\* \* \*

With the taste of bacon still in his mouth, Torey is all smiles as he paddles back out into the ocean. This time he is on his favorite shortboard.

Waves are still rolling in with consistent sets, and the June Gloom is nonexistent today. Torey can almost clearly see Donovan about two hundred yards out waiting for him, still holding his old harpoon. *What's up with that?* Torey wonders. Yet he cannot wait to talk to him. He redoubles his strokes.

Donovan greets him. "Look at you, all smiles and carefree."

"What, I can't be happy?" Torey retorts.

"That is not your everyday, everything is normal smile," The old surfer remarks. "I'm thinking that your schoolmates are treating you with a little more respect after your big fight. Maybe stepping out of your way to let you pass. Perhaps they are even-"

"I was on a date," Torey blurts out.

This is more than Donovan had expected. He grins. "Dude, it's like I don't even know you anymore. Is she-?"

Torey smiles. "Oh yes."

"Well look at you. Too cool for school." Donovan initiates a fist bump.

"Yeah it's cool and all, and everyone is happy that I took the twins down a notch, but nobody knows what to think of me. They still keep their distance from me and-"

Donovan cuts him off. "So did I make you cool, or do we still have some work to do?"

Torey has no frame of reference as to how cool he really is, so he simply nods.

"Have you had any luck with dynamism yet?" Donovan asks.

"I created a water funnel this morning."

"This morning? You were out this morning?" Donovan asks.

"Yeah, I was too stoked to sleep and I couldn't just lay there with my eyes open. I looked for you, but you must have been sleeping."

Donovan laughs. "Well, I will just have to set my alarm clock a little earlier."

Torey knows full well that Donovan doesn't have an alarm clock. He doesn't bother to respond.

They both shut up for a moment to rise up with and let a nice swell sweep by. They watch it become a wave and roll its way to a satisfying crash along the shoreline.

Torey is the first to break the silence. "So there are waves again?"

## 3. Rafferty

"It took me and three mermaids all we had to shut down the surf," Donovan admits. "To tell you the truth, it is pretty freaking exhausting. Besides, it's time to make you cool beyond your wildest dreams. Everyone at school will want to be your friend."

Torey frowns. "But what if I don't want to be everyone's friend?"

"That, my boy, is one of the perks of being cool- you get to pick and choose your friends. Just try to not be too cruel. Cruel is not cool."

"Everyone thinks the Appalling Twins are cool."

Donovan can hardly believe that he actually has to address this issue. "Are the twins cool or are they feared? Everyone wants to hang with the cool kids. No one wants to hang out with bullies."

This thought blows Torey's mind. *The Appalling Twins aren't cool.* He realizes that Donovan is correct. "I should probably feel sorry for them," he responds thoughtfully.

Donovan finds this amusing. "Damn kid, it's survival of the fittest. You do what you have to do as long as you end up on top. Remember that."

Torey commits this piece of advice to memory. "So what now?"

Donovan doesn't answer right away. He is quickly running out of time. The portal that allows him to sneak out of his hell is showing signs of weakness, but he figures that he has at least a couple weeks before it collapses. He fears that he doesn't have the mental fortitude to rebuild it again and must move quickly, cut corners and take giant steps. "Are there any type of surfing competitions around here?"

Torey jumps on this idea. "There is a Pro-Am competition next Saturday, up at Huntington Beach. There'll be sponsors there and everything." Torey is psyched at the thought of it. "But they might cancel it due to the lack of surf."

Donovan cuts him off. "There will be waves again from now on through the competition. Just be sure that you sign up for it. When you win it, you will no doubt become the epitome of cool."

Torey looks at Donovan suspiciously. "Win it? I don't want to win it by cheating."

"Cheating?" Donovan says with a mock hurt tone of voice. "I will only set you up with a killer wave. The rest is all up to you. Better yet, work on your dynamism and you can do it all by yourself." Donovan adds, "Besides, cheaters are not cool."

Torey loves the thought of being in a competition. He even imagines that maybe he can win it. Donovan is impatient for an answer. "Are we cool with this?"

"We are so cool with this."

They ride a couple of waves together until other surfers realize that there are waves again and rush the beach. Donovan catches Torey's attention and winks, then disappears below the surface.

Torey spends the rest of the day lined up for sets with dozens of other surfers.

The surf is back at Dana Point!

* * *

It is late afternoon and the beaches of Southern California are packed to capacity. It is a perfect beach day with a cool breeze that makes the eighty-five degree heat seem comfortable. Billowy clouds dapple the sky but are in no position to block the sun.

Torey cannot believe he is actually surfed out. He steps over and around beach blankets and sunbathers. After surfing through the early morning hours on the longboard and the rest of the day on his shortboard, he is happily exhausted.

## . Rafferty

Torey signed up for the surf contest at a local surf shop and decides to relax for a bit. He chooses an empty spot between an elderly couple who watch the surfers and a mother with five-year-old twin girls and a three-year-old boy. The mother attempts to read a novel despite her children's constant bickering and vying for her attention as they shape what appears to be a lumpy sand castle.

Torey spreads out a beach towel with a faded print of a sailfish catching air. He lies back with a comfortable sigh and closes his eyes. Despite being physically tired, his mind is occupied with three different lines of thought. The upcoming surf competition has him running possible scenarios and outcomes. He is also still replaying every moment of his date with Cassandra, along with the nagging thought, *Why didn't I ask her for her phone number?* And as if these competing thoughts were not enough, he still can't understand why his dynamism over water is so weak and not responding to his wishes.

Torey decides to practice moving air for now. He looks up at a puffy cloud and focuses his thoughts on it. He imagines that it extends and shape shifts as if he were drawing on his schoolbook covers. The cloud begins to change form; suddenly one end of it resembles a rough looking fish tail. The other end of the cloud slowly but surely pivots upwards. It is taking a crude form of a mermaid, but it would take someone with great imagination to see it.

He goes to work on the finer details of his creation. The mermaid's arms separate from her body. Her hair splays out in splendid long waves. Her feminine form grows and becomes more defined.

The old dude on the blanket next to him points excitedly. He wants his wife to stop eyeing the surfers for a second and look up at the sky.

"Dang it Myrtle, just look at that cloud and tell me that isn't a mermaid."

Torey relaxes his concentration and lets the cloud collapse in on itself to a more naturally billowy formation.

"I don't see any mermaid, you silly fart," the old dude's wife says.

The twin girls next to him are screaming at their younger brother who has knocked over a large section of their castle. "Mommy. Mommy! Mikey ruined it! Mommy?"

Mommy is apparently at a juicy chapter of her book. She shushes them as they surround her. The two girls continue yelling and the little boy is now crying from all the yelling. Everyone in the vicinity tries his or her best to ignore the irritating scene.

Torey looks at the mound of sand and wishes that he could just fix the castle in order to get these kids to quiet down. No sooner does the thought enter his mind that the sand instantly transforms its mass into a majestic castle with high turrets and an arched bridge that spans a moat. Stonework is even etched around the windows. The girls yell even louder now.

"Mommy, look what Mikey did!"

Mom finally tears her attention away from the book and beholds the spectacular castle with a gasp.

"Mikey! You built that? I have to get a picture." She turns to find her cell phone.

All three children squeal with delight and simultaneously rush the castle and jump on it, smashing it down with the weight of their bodies. They happily roll on the now shapeless mound of sand.

The mother is stunned with a drop-jawed expression on her face. She looks around to see if anyone else saw what she saw. The elderly couple is looking up at the sky. Torey pretends that he saw nothing and does not acknowledge her.

*But I hardly even thought to do that.* Torey is startled by how easily it all happened. But then it hits him, *Earth? How can I have dynamism over Earth? Why not water?* He feels distressed. This means that I have no control over water at all. But I love the water. This doesn't make any sense.

Oddly, his confidence is shaken by this newfound ability to manipulate earth. *Dirt,* he thinks, *I have spent my entire life trying to get off of dirt and into the water. How can I not have dynamism over water?*

Then he recalls having some success moving his board in the water. *Maybe I have three dynamisms? Or maybe Donovan moved the water to... to... because he didn't really believe that I could do it.*

His thoughts are suddenly suspicious and scattered all over the place. He can no longer think straight. These kids are so freaking loud, and this old man won't stop yelling at his hard-of-hearing wife to see the mermaid cloud, which by now looks more like a corndog.

Torey feels mentally and physically exhausted. Nothing makes any sense to him. He desperately needs somebody to talk to. He wonders if he can talk to Cassandra about dynamism without freaking her out and scaring her off. *But I forgot to get her number!* And he can't tell Donovan that he can't move water. He is suddenly anxious to get off the sand. He grabs his towel and steps his way over and around blankets and sunbathers. His only thoughts are to lie down in his bed and take a nap.

# Chapter 9
# *Like Blisters In The Sun*

It is Sunday afternoon and Torey wakes with a start. *Why is it so bright in here?* He jumps out of bed and throws on yesterday's clothes before rushing to the living room where his mom sits by the window admiring the view.

Torey is still half asleep and one hundred percent disoriented. "What time is it?"

"It's one thirty," his mom tells him.

"One thirty? What day is it?"

His brain finally grasps that he has slept through half of Sunday. "Why didn't you wake me?"

"It's normal for an adolescent boy to need more sleep. Your body expends so much energy just growing."

Torey wonders if Donovan would buy this excuse. "I'm going surfing."

"You are not going anywhere until you eat your breakfast," she tells him.

"I don't have time for breakfast."

"Then you will just have to settle for lunch." She stands and heads for the kitchen.

* * *

It is three o'clock and Torey is just past the breakers. A surfer or two wave as he approaches. He waves back and surprises them by paddling past them and out to the deep waters.

Donovan is nowhere to be found. Torey swims out with long purposeful strokes until he hears a teasing voice behind him.

"Where are you going?"

Torey stops paddling and sits upright on his board and turns to face Donovan. The surfers behind him appear the size of ants. The shoreline is indiscernible.

"I don't know what happened. It's so freaking late."

Donovan can read the sense of panic on his face. "Calm down, dude."

"I am calm."

"No, you aren't."

"I slept until one thirty," Torey says in a freaked out tone of voice. "I have never slept past eight o'clock."

"Yeah well it happens, kid. I can almost remember experiencing the same thing when I was your age. Your body is developing and making incredible demands on your energy. I'm actually surprised that this is the first time that you overslept."

Torey finally allows his mind to stop racing. "That's what my mom said." He checks his surroundings and realizes just how far from shore he paddled.

Donovan notices his concern. "We'll drift back as we talk."

Torey can feel the sudden change in the current. He tries to urge it to pull faster, but does not feel he has any influence on it at all. This failure to move the water has him frustrated.

"You told me that the mermaid tricked you and that you woke up in hell," he says.

Donovan waits for him to finish asking the question.

"So how do you know about Dynamism? Did you know about these things when you lived on land, or was it after you woke up in hell that you figured it out?"

Donovan has never been asked this before. In fact, Torey is the first person that he has spoken to in a long time. Not including the poor sap that freaked out and had a heart attack and drowned when he popped up beside him a few weeks ago. He doesn't know the answer to this question, so he tells Torey the truth.

"I don't know. I have thought about this very question quite a lot. I mean, when I woke up in that terrible place every nerve in my body screamed in pain, and I was disoriented and confused. Rage ruled the day. The love of my life was not at my side. There were strange voices in my head and some of them were really vicious.

"I had unfamiliar memories as well. Memories of places I had never been to, and of things that I could not remember having done. Terrible things. I felt that I was half myself and half someone else. I had memories to substantiate multiple personalities, but I could not figure out where one ended and the other began. Like Dr. Jekyll and Mr. Hyde, except both were awake at the same time. I felt like the real me was buried somewhere deep inside struggling to regain control, but something dark took over who I once was. Eventually my own personality began to regain some control, but I still couldn't figure out what I did that was so terrible that I deserved to be trapped in that infernal place."

The sea gets choppy as he recounts what happened to him. "I don't know how I know about these things," he tells Torey, "but one of the mermaids that is trapped in there with me saw me desperately trying to influence the water. Perhaps she took pity on me. She helped me develop my skills."

"Maybe she was bored," Torey says trying to lighten the conversation.

"What?"

"Maybe she helped you because she had nothing else to do."

The sea gets even choppier. "Maybe you should shut up."

Torey is concerned that Donovan is once again unable to control his anger. He feels somewhat relieved that they have drifted a little closer to shore.

* * *

Meanwhile, back on land, Byron pulls his new pre-owned hearse that he recently found on the internet into the beach parking lot. "I know, I have to get the AC checked out," he assures Cassandra. "The dude that sold it to me failed to mention that it didn't work. And why are we here?"

"I wish I knew. It's just… it's just… I don't know." Cassandra steps out of Byron's car and into the sunlight. Her black clothes suck in the sun's heat and she is visibly uncomfortable. Her plastic water bottle is already empty. She recalls a time when she had the sense to wear light comfortable clothing on a hot day.

Byron stands beside her in his signature black overcoat. He pops opens a black umbrella and says, "It doesn't really matter. I am here to accompany you on this strange path upon which you have chosen to walk. Let us just hope that we can find our way back."

Cassandra stares blankly at Byron for a moment then turns her attention to the beach and the water. A memory of her twelve-year-old self jumping happily into the waves floods her overheated mind. She considers that it might be a good idea, despite wearing layers of lacy black clothing, to do that now.

"I know this sounds strange, but I want to see him..." she edits herself, "...surf."

Cassandra fully realizes that if any of her friends behaved like she is behaving, she would totally call them out on it. But this is her and she can't explain her actions, except that nothing has been the same for her since she kissed Torey. "I'll be okay. Maybe you can pick me up in an hour or so?"

Byron is convinced that she is going through some weird phase. Trolling the beach to see some wannabe surfer nerd ride a wave is definitely not her style. But he considers himself to be her best friend and will be damned if he lets her wander the beach alone. He hands her the umbrella and pulls out another one from the back of his coffin cart.

"Don't be silly," he says, "I will not be leaving you alone this day in this strange land."

Cassandra rolls her eyes but can't help but smile. She is glad for the company.

Two goths strolling across the hot sand carrying black umbrellas is not an everyday sight at any beach in South California, let alone a Dana Point beach. They are attracting a lot of attention. Cassandra is too busy checking the surfers in her search for Torey to notice the attention they are getting.

"Do you see him?" she asks.

Byron squints into the surf. "They all look the same to me."

He points farther out, "Maybe he's one of those guys way out there."

She puts her hand to her face to shield her eyes from the sun, but the glare is too strong to tell who it is.

\* \* \*

Torey and Donovan have drifted back to about fifty yards behind the line of surfers. He now regrets having asked Donovan how he knows about dynamism. He never expected that it would put him in such a foul mood. Donovan even just admitted that he has multiple personalities. *He's like a schizo or something.*

Donovan motions his finger to a wave that a surfer is riding. The wave reverses its curl unnaturally and sends the hapless surfer over the falls and into a serious wipeout.

"What's with you?"

Donovan ignores Torey's question as the sight of two vampires walking along the beach has caught his attention. "Are you freaking kidding me?"

He stares, trying to reason this out. Torey follows his gaze and sees Cassandra. His heart skips a beat.

"What the hell am I looking at?" Donovan asks.

Torey becomes embarrassed by Donovan's tone of voice and decides against telling him that this is the girl that he has a crush on. "They are goths, they…"

Donovan has a new target to vent his anger on. "Hey kid, check this out."

He raises both of his hands and moves his fingers in a counter-clockwise circular motion. The umbrellas on the beach quiver as a strong breeze suddenly picks up.

\* \* \*

Dillon and the Appalling twins relax on the sand after a round of skimboarding. The unexpected breeze momentarily relieves everyone from the heat, but as it steadily increases in intensity, people cringe from being blasted by sand.

Suddenly a beach umbrella uproots and is blown end over end along the beach. Two more umbrellas follow its lead. They topple erratically and catch big air. There are yells of warning as sunbathers scramble to get out of their paths. Everyone else with umbrellas still planted in the sand scramble to collapse them before they can take flight as well.

Dillon is the first to act. He runs to intercept the closest umbrella as it heads straight for him. He dives for the wooden pole and grabs it just shy of the spike and manages to wrestle it down before it can go any further.

Meanwhile, the twins, who were inspired by Dillon, chase down a second runaway umbrella. Simon has a better angle to cut it off. He hurdles a couple on a blanket to make his move. He sets his stance and braces himself for the grab, but wind-blown umbrellas don't tumble in a predictable manner. It takes a funny hop and the canopy end of it nails Simon in the chest, but he manages to slow it down just long enough for Sidney to grab the pole and collapse it.

Dillon jogs over to them. He reaches down to offer a hand to Simon. Everyone at the beach applauds the three heroes.

A third umbrella is still on a rampage and is toppling along the water line safely past the crowd, but is heading directly for Cassandra and Byron.

Dillon yells to, "Look out!" But the wind is too fierce to let a mere voice carry through. He and the twins attempt to cut off the stampeding umbrella, but it is too late. They all yell to get the goths' attention.

Cassandra and Byron are unaware of the turmoil. They have braced their backs against the wind, but they continue to squint against the sun in an attempt to find Torey.

Torey does not find it at all amusing and yells at Donovan to "Stop it! Stop what you are doing!" His yelling does no good so he pushes Donovan off his board.

Donovan does not miss a beat. He keeps his deadly focus while steadying his board between himself and Torey so that Torey can't get another shot at him.

"We are about to find out if a wooden stake is really what it takes to kill a vampire," he announces with reckless glee.

Torey watches helplessly as the stampeding umbrella catches air. It does a double flip end over end, just as Byron turns to see it head straight for his chest.

Torey feels helpless until his reflexes take over. He motions with his fingers to manipulate the air against Donovan's control.

Everyone on the beach gasps with horror as the umbrella plows into Byron and takes him down. The wind relents as soon as the spike of the umbrella buries itself into the poor unsuspecting goth.

Cassandra screams, "Byron!"

Dillon slides beside Byron a moment later. "Somebody call nine-one-one!"

It appears that the spike has pierced through Byron's chest and has planted itself deep into the sand. The twins arrive and immediately move to pull the stake out. Dillon stops them.

"How you doing Pal?"

Byron responds weakly, "I think I'm okay."

Sidney gasps whispers to his brother, "Shouldn't a stake in the heart kill a vampire?"

"It should probably kill anybody," Simon answers.

Cassandra takes her friend's arm and gently pulls it away from his side. She laughs out loud with a flood of relief. "You lucky son-of-a-bitch." She rocks away from him and back onto her feet.

A crowd has now formed and before long everyone understands the joke. The spike had pierced the space between Byron's arm and his rib cage.

Byron shrugs off his overcoat as he rises shakily. He peels off his black tee shirt to check for damage. Everyone can see, despite the glare of his pasty white skin, that his encounter with the wooden stake has left him with only a nasty red rash on his side and the inside of his arm.

Simon mock punches Byron's shoulder. "Dude, you scared the crap out of us!"

Everyone who has crowded around laugh with shared relief. Byron can't help but laugh along with them. For this brief moment in time, surfer boys, bullies, goths, and sun worshippers of all ages share a moment of camaraderie.

Torey is greatly relieved, but his anger with Donovan takes precedence. "Are you crazy? You could have killed someone!"

Now that the moment has passed Donovan finds that he is able to regain control over the wave of rage that had consumed him. He pulls himself from the water and sits calmly astride his board.

"Dude, what is wrong with you?"

Donovan stares back at Torey with an expression of bemused calmness. All evidence of his crazed anger has vanished. "It's cool," he says, and congratulates Torey with a sincere smile. "It doesn't work if you think too hard about it, but a sense of urgency can do wonders to quickly develop your dynamism. You, my boy, get a gold star."

"Wait? What? That was a test?" Torey is not ready to accept this. *He was really going to kill Byron…or was he?*

Conflicting thoughts fight out a virtual cage match in his mind. He exhales sharply in an attempt to calm down despite the flood of adrenaline that still flows through his veins.

Donovan and his board sink into the water. "I will see you on Saturday at the tournament, kid. Until then, take it easy. Keep an eye out for my mermaid and get to know your new girlfriend."

"But what if I couldn't have saved them?"

"But you did save them," counters Donovan. All but his head are beneath the surface.

Before his lips hit the water, he adds, "Your next lesson will be on mermaid hunting."

He winks at Torey and disappears from sight.

"You crazy bastard," Torey says to the water.

He lies down on his board and paddles with long strokes. He is anxious to see how Cassandra is doing. At the moment he feels anything but confident. He doesn't know what he is going to say to her. She must be so freaked out.

He catches a wave and rides it the rest of the way to shore. Despite his worries, he can't help but make the most of the wave and cut across its lip. He jumps the rim and catches air. He thinks that he hears Cassandra yell out a "Woo!" for his efforts as he rides the swell and foam the rest of the way in.

Torey cannot believe his eyes when Cassandra wades out fully dressed into the knee-deep water to greet him.

"Look at you, surfer boy," she grabs his shoulders with both hands. She looks into Torey's eyes and flashes an intense smile.

Torey is instantly relieved. *She is definitely not a mermaid!* He doesn't think he could deal with something like that, but for now his predominant thought is that he wants to kiss her. Cassandra wants him to kiss her, too.

Torey chickens out. Instead he asks, "Are you okay?"

She is more than okay. She is full of energy. She is ecstatic. "Now I understand why you like the beach so much. It's so full of energy and randomness. And I forgot what it is like to be in the ocean. I am so glad that I finally found you."

"I was thinking I was a dumbass for not getting your phone number."

She laughs. "It's not like I gave you much of a chance."

Torey takes her hand and walks her back up to the group. "Boy, that was close, Byron." *What if I couldn't save have saved him?*

Byron has quickly regained his well-practiced indifference. "Welcome to my life." He kneels down in the sand to study the damage to his prized coat.

Torey strides up to Simon and Sidney and says, "I saw you guys take out that umbrella. That was really cool of you."

Simon holds his fist in its normal clenched position. Torey reaches out and fist bumps it. Simon immediately rubs his hand as if wiping off cooties.

Sidney is not going to be friendly with the dork. And for the rest of his life, he will never tell anyone that he always had a crush on Cassandra, but was too afraid of girls to ask her out. He punches Simon's shoulder for no reason.

"Later," he says, and they head back to where they left their skimboards.

Dillon watches the twins leave then turns to face Torey and Cassandra. "You do understand that you two are going to blow many minds?"

This is the first time that Torey and Cassandra have considered *"us two."* Cassandra slips her arm around his waist and pulls him close. She laughs as his form fits hers perfectly. "People will just have to get over it."

Dillon shakes his head then fist bumps each of them. He turns and walks away to give them their space.

Cassandra looks into Torey's eyes and asks coyly, "So are you going to teach me to surf or what?"

"Now?" he asks.

"Yes, now. Is there a problem with that?"

"That's a lot of clothing for surfing, but okay."

He leads her into hip deep water and helps her lay down onto the board.

"A wave is coming. You are going to duck dive under it."

"What is a duck dive?"

The wave rolls in and Torey guides the board under and through it.

"Oh," she exclaims as she resurfaces and whips her now drenched long black hair over her shoulder. Black lines of wet mascara and eyeliner run down her face. "Duck dive. Good to know."

Torey leads her further out. He spins her around and says, "Here comes a pretty good wave, I will guide you into it. Just stay down and enjoy the ride and get a feel for it."

As the wave rolls in, Torey guides Cassandra into it and sends her on her way.

Cassandra does not want to just lie down like a boogie boarder. She gets up onto her knees, but she does not know what to do next. She rides it until the wave runs its course and curls over and foams out. She laughs from the pure joy of this simple moment.

Torey is all smiles as Cassandra lies back down on the board and paddles to him. She shifts and sits on the board as she approaches him as if she has done it a hundred times before. "I didn't stand up! I didn't know what to do!"

"Do you want to stand now or wait for next time?" He asks teasingly.

She says to him in a mock surfer voice, "Dude, we are like not leaving this beach until I ride a gnarly wave fer sure." More genuinely, she is getting caught up in the feeling of freedom that surfing offers.

Torey thinks about how best to explain it to her. He has been doing this since he was three years old and never actually had to think about it. He looks into her gorgeous green eyes and explains, "Remember when you were a kid, lying on the floor and watching television?"

"Yes, of course."

"Well, just imagine that you are lying down on the floor and your mom calls you for dinner- jump up and go."

Cassandra replays the scenario in her head. "I can do that." She looks past Torey and tells him, "Not this one. The second one."

Torey can appreciate the wave that she chose, and that she even thought to choose one. He lets the first one pass. "Ready?"

She nods her head yes. It is a perfect wave for a newbie and Torey releases the board as the wave sweeps by.

Cassandra gains speed. "You are so mine," she announces to the wave and springs up like her mom just called her for dinner.

*I'm standing!* It feels as if she is moving too fast and in slow motion at the same time. She does not know what to do next, so she simply raises her hands and screams with pure adrenaline-charged delight.

Everyone on the beach can't help but smile at the sight of a beautiful young woman in a soaking wet, layered black lace dress riding her first wave and laughing as she wipes out. Torey cheers her on and makes a mental note that she is a goofy foot (a surfer who rides right foot forward; surf-speak for a lefty).

\* \* \*

Meanwhile, Byron sits passively on the beach with his knees pulled up to his chest. He is itchy from the sand and uncomfortable in the sun. With the passing of every shadow he twists defensively to see if another damn umbrella is bearing down at him. *I can't wait to get off this hellhole of a beach,* he complains to himself crankily.

He watches Cassandra and regrets taking her here. *What was I thinking?* He wonders why it took him so long to realize he loves her. He took her for granted for too long. Byron does not want to lose her.

*Let her have her fun,* he thinks selfishly, *tomorrow she will regret this undertaking with a third-degree sunburn. The lovely pale complexion that she has spent years to perfect will be marred by a disgusting tan and hideous peeling skin.* He feels better already.

He waves meekly to her, but she does not notice his lame wave. She is already pushing the surfboard back towards Torey.

\* \* \*

Cassandra couldn't suppress her ear-to-ear grin if she tried. Torey wades in to meet her halfway. He is blown away by how well she did, and by how happy she is. He raises his hand for a celebratory high five.

*Oh, he thinks that this is a high five moment, does he?* She raises her hand to meet his and intertwines their fingers. She presses her wet body against his and plants a tender and passionate kiss full on Torey's lips.

*Bam!*

Torey's mind is blank to everything; he isn't even aware that his toes have curled into feet fists. The feel of her sensual lips pressed firmly against his, the inhale of her sweet breath into his mouth, the touch of her hand on his shoulder, and her other hand still holding his above their heads. A kiss that seems to last an eternity, yet ends way too soon.

This is not Cassandra's first kiss, but she never experienced the jolt of electricity that happens when she kisses Torey. Every cell in her body is startled awake with a blissful surge of energy. She thought that she was just having a good time with a weird surfer boy. In this moment, she knows that this will not be their last kiss. This is to be one of many kisses with a surfer boy who is quickly becoming a surfer man.

*What have I done?* Cassandra wonders briefly as she hugs Torey tightly and presses the side of her cool, pale face against his warm, tan shoulder. If she could think clearly, she might be concerned with the impact this will have on her social standing when her friends find out she is dating Torey. But she isn't thinking clearly. Her thoughts are clouded with love and she knows it. She embraces every bit of this perfect moment in time. Distracting thoughts can wait until tomorrow.

\* \* \*

Donovan has been quietly watching Torey and this odd girl the entire time. Only his eyes break the surface, even though it is a risk that a surfer may come too close and spot him. *The boy's taste in women is quite unexpected.* He concedes that nothing in his life makes sense anymore so why should anything in Torey's life make any sense either?

He has seen enough for one day. It's time to go back and spend some time toiling to bring order to the chaos in his little corner of hell.

# Chapter 10
## *Strange Days Indeed*

Torey was awake for most of the night, thinking about Cassandra and kissing her. He wakes up knowing that he overslept again and that there is no way that he is going to catch the bus. He yells into the house, "Dad, you have to drive me to school." He catches a whiff of bacon.

"Uh, you know I don't like that stink in the house," he hears his mom complain loudly,

"The kid overslept two days in a row," his dad answers. "He obviously needs protein."

She half laughs a response. "That is just your excuse to stuff your own face with swine."

His mom yells again, this time to Torey, "Check your closet for the new clothes that I bought for you."

"We leave in ten minutes, kiddo," his dad also calls out.

Torey is disoriented. *Bacon, twice in two days? And mom bought me new clothes?*

Torey has a sinking feeling about what kind of bargain basement nightmare will be waiting for him when he looks in the closet.

He swings the door open and to his surprise, three brand new shirts hang from the rail. He is shocked. "Did you buy these at a surf shop? These are awesome!"

"Yes. Put on the blue and green plaid shirt and the leather sandals."

Torey looks down and sure enough, there is a box with a new pair of Reef sandals. *What is going on?*

"Did we win the lottery?"

"And don't forget to comb your hair," his mom replies.

This is the type of clothes that Torey always had to wait a year or two until the price dropped enough for his parents to afford. He pops the tags off the shirt and tries it on for size.

His parents check him out as he steps into the kitchen. His mom smiles approvingly as she adjusts his collar and brushes his hair with her fingers. "Look at my son, all grown up." She kisses his cheek.

Torey is just happy that she is in such a good mood, and appears to be healthy again. He doesn't want to question it, but can't help but ask, "Is it my birthday?" He grins at his mom.

His dad slaps a toast and bacon sandwich into his hand. "C'mon or you'll be late."

His mom presses a napkin into his other hand. "Be sure that you don't mess up your new shirt."

His days just keep getting stranger and stranger as he is ushered to the jeep. "Wait, I forgot my books."

"They are on the back seat," his dad tells him. "Lets go."

His dad whistles a classic Dick Dale tune as only he can while they drive up the Pacific Coast Highway. Torey waits for his father to finish whistling his version of Wipe Out before asking, "Really, what is going on?"

The Beachcomber grins as he slows to let a car pull out in front of him, "Isn't it obvious? Your mom got wind that you got yourself a girlfriend."

"Yeah, I mean, but... why the...?"

"It's a big deal for your mom," he says. "This is new ground... for you, and she is excited about...well...let's just say that she is really happy and leave it at that. Sound good?"

Torey thinks that it has been almost a month since he has seen his mom really happy. He really missed her bubbly personality. If wearing new clothes is what it will take to bring back her old self, then he would be more than happy to oblige.

* * *

The goths at Dick Dale High are gathered at their usual spot in the school's lobby. Byron's face is red and nearly well done from all of the sun he caught yesterday. He tries to substantiate or deny all the rumors that the others have been hearing.

"No, it didn't pierce my heart. Yes, Cassandra went surfing. No, she isn't wearing flowery sundresses," he snorts back a derisive laugh. "Yes, she..." he doesn't want to say it.

"Did she or didn't she?" They need to know.

For Byron, the very question is intolerable, but at least they can share in his misery. "Yes. She kissed the surfer boy."

The goths gasp, some from disgust and indignity, others with excitement.

"It's like a fairytale romance," says one of the girls. "Like Beauty and the Beast, only stranger."

"Just remember that she will be as hideously burnt as I am," Byron says as he gingerly touches his red cheek. "And I am sure that she greatly regrets her actions of yesterday as much as I do. So let us agree to not be too harsh on her. Though it would be more than appropriate if we don't let her off too easy."

"Hi guys," she startles them.

Cassandra is not sunburned. Her skin isn't peeling. In fact, she is radiant. She still wears all black, but only those close to her would realize that she has shed a couple layers and that her clothes are of a more modern flair than gothic. She sports a tight fitting, long sleeve cropped tee paired with a long flowing black skirt and completes the ensemble with knee-high black leather gladiator sandals.

"I am so going shopping after school," a sophomore goth named Claudia (pronounced "Cloudy-a") exclaims.

Byron is beside himself. "Why aren't you sunburned?"

"My mom is the queen of the tan. She knows all the tricks to dealing with too much sun. By the way, she gave me this to give to you." She hands him a bottle of green aloe vera gel.

Byron pulls his hand back as if it was garlic. "What would I want with that?"

She looks him in the eye. "You can either soothe your burn with this gel, or you can go with the crispy and peely look of an unfortunate extra in a horror movie. It's your call."

Byron reluctantly accepts the gel but says accusingly, "You're getting a tan. It shows through your makeup."

Cassandra frowns. She hasn't wrapped her mind around that yet. "Maybe tan and laid-back is the new pale and uptight."

Byron has no ready answer for such sacrilege. He is about to say something completely ridiculous when Claudia exclaims, "Is that him?"

Byron follows her line of sight and sees Torey. Something seems different about him. He strides through the doorway knowing that his bully problems are a thing of the past. But it is more than that. He has swagger in his step. Swagger!

Cassandra turns to see Torey approaching in his stylish new threads. "I don't know about you guys, but I am ready to step out of my comfort zone," she tells her friends.

Cassandra turns and embraces Torey. As she kisses him, she deftly peels the size sticker off of the side of his sleeve.

"I suddenly feel overdressed," Claudia announces. She rolls her black stockings down from under her leather skirt and tucks them into her knee-high boots.

Byron groans. "This is not good."

She proceeds to tie her blouse at the midriff. "This feels so much better," she exclaims.

"That is so not cool," Byron hisses.

"You look awesome," Cassandra tells Torey. She places her hand over his eyes, and asks playfully, "What am I wearing?"

"I have no idea what you are wearing," Torey answers, "but your smile is as bright as sunshine."

At that moment she realizes that he sees her for being her. *I could wear a potato sack and he would be happy to see me.*

"When did you get to be so smooth?" she whispers in his ear.

Torey has been called a lot of things: he has been called a

nerd, a dork, a dumb-ass grom, a wannabe...but he has never been called smooth. He simply smiles and says, "I'm entered in the Huntington Beach Pro-Am on Saturday."

"Are you going to win it?"

He laughs. "Win it? It will be cool just to catch a few waves and be a part of it. I have never entered a competition before."

"Well, I will be sure to get there early and grab a sweet view from the pier," she promises.

The thought that she will be there makes Torey's eyes smile. "Your presence will do wonders for my nerves."

She frowns. *Does he mean that he doesn't want me there?*

"Oh please, if you don't want me there I will totally understand."

"What? No! I meant that in a good way. I definitely want you there!"

Cassandra purrs. "Now that that's settled, let's get to homeroom and make out in front of Nussman."

Torey laughs out loud. She laughs along with him and leans her body close to his as they walk.

The fact that Cassandra and Torey are dating has not gone unnoticed. The Queen of the Goths is dating a boy outside of her social clique. In what demented parallel universe does that happen?

The student body's perception of the current structure of cliques has suddenly come into question. Some wonder how long it will be before Torey starts wearing all black clothing and growing fangs. A cheerleader is overheard asking her friends if they would ever consider dating a goth or even somebody from another clique.

Torey and Cassandra inadvertently created a ripple effect on the school's social fabric. Even Claudia felt encouraged and invited herself to sit at lunch with cheerleaders; she always had a secret longing to be a member of the pep squad. The cheerleaders were taken aback at first, but they began asking what being goth was all about.

By Friday, Nick, the quarterback of the school team, was so sick of hearing about the goth dating the surfer dude that he and one of his teammates decided to come to school wearing their traditional pre-game jerseys. Only this time, they also wore goth-inspired makeup, including black eyeliner and lipstick, to make a point about how ridiculous this has all become. The plan was to freak out their girlfriends so they could get back to talking about more important things, like parties and cars and football.

But they decided to take things one step further. During gym class, they pretended they wanted to recruit Byron Toomey as a kicker for the team.

"Our punter pulled his groin during practice, and you have long legs, so we figure you are our best hope." They stifle their laughter as they pressure Byron into kicking footballs.

Byron finally relents. "If I kick one of your stupid balls, will you leave me alone?"

They assure him mockingly, "Sure, just give it a shot. Surely you can kick it a couple of yards." They toss him a ball.

Byron regards them with contempt. He takes three steps and punts the ball hard as if it was one of their heads. The ball flies a good thirty yards. The football players are stunned.

"Count Chocula got leg."

"That ball actually had good hang time."

"That was beginner's luck," Nick tells Byron. "I'll give you ten bills if you can do that again."

Byron exhales loudly, then proceeds to punt the ball even further than his first attempt. Coach Boyle had been watching silently from the bleachers until he had seen enough. He shakes his head as he approaches the three. He asks Nick, "What are you thinking?"

The two players expect to be balled out for dressing like vampires. Nick replies, "We just dressed like this to make a point–"

"There is no way that he is going to be ready for tomorrow's game."

"We weren't serious, we were just messing around," Nick protests.

Coach Boyle jabs a finger into his chest. "For tomorrow, you just make sure that we don't need to punt. What's with the vampire crap?"

"Like I said, we were just trying to make a point," Nick says.

Coach Boyle suddenly feels inspired. "Yes, lets make a point. I want you two clowns dressed like this for tomorrow's game."

He turns to Byron. "Well, Adam Vampiteri, we will see you at practice on Monday. Bring your own cup." The coach is the only one to chuckle at, or even get, his lame joke.

"Wait. What?" Byron protests.

"Hey, we didn't mean–," Nick starts, but the coach is already walking off the field.

Byron groans. *What has this ridiculous jock gotten me into?*

It has been a rough week for Byron. He waited too long to express his true feelings for Cassandra, and now he is being dragged out of his insulated world and into sports of all things.

He will admit to himself, however, that it did feel good to kick something.

\* \* \*

After school is for surfing. Cassandra strides along the beach wearing a black wetsuit with short sleeves and pant legs. She knows this will be a prolonged surf lesson and she does not want to take the chance of cutting it short with chattering teeth. She beams when she sees that Torey has brought two boards today, his usual plus a shorter twin-fin board that is better suited for someone of Cassandra's weight and build. He spent all night drawing on it with a sharpie marker: a gothic-styled picture of Cassandra's head sitting atop crossed bones and black roses.

"I love it!" She kisses him for at least the tenth time of the day.

Torey is relieved. "I'm not sure I did you justice, but I felt inspired."

"You are damn right you felt inspired," she chides him. "Why are we standing here? Let's break it in."

They paddle out to the line up next to other surfers as they have every day this week. The other surfers consider Cassandra to be a "freakdudette" and give her a hard time, but she doesn't let it get to her. The surfers are beginning to realize that she is serious about surfing and that she won't take any of their crap, but they are not completely comfortable with a goth surfer chick yet.

Cassandra doesn't care either way. She is focused on catching this next wave that is quickly approaching. "You guys take this one. I'll get the next," she tells two other surfers.

They hesitate to see why the next wave is better, but she takes the wave. It's her first ride on the smaller board and she immediately feels that she has more control. She rides the wave, gaining more momentum than she has ever experienced, and decides that she is going to try to catch air like Torey does. She cuts back up the wave to jump the lip. She catches air, but the wave passes by, leaving her to drop not-so-smoothly back into the water.

Cassandra swims to her board and climbs back on in time to watch Torey catch the next wave. Not only does he catch air, he completes a three-sixty and sticks the landing. She takes a mental note that he grabbed the edge of the board with one hand while he spun, but she doesn't know how the wave didn't pass him by. As he paddles back to her she yells out, "You have to teach me that, you showoff."

"I can't believe you tried an aerial! And you actually caught air! It took me two years to get the nerve to try an aerial." He recalls the moment and doesn't think that his board actually left the water.

They spend some time floating in the shallows critiquing other surfers trying aerials. Torey explains exactly how they pulled it off, or what they did to earn a wipeout. "There is still some light left. Do you want to give it another try?"

"No," Cassandra answers, "I would rather float here and watch the sunset with my boyfriend on the night before his big competition."

Torey moves close to her and puts his arm around her waist. She laughs and slips out of his embrace to paddle towards the break.

Of course she is going to give it another try.

Cassandra straddles her board next to the two remaining surfers. She calls the oncoming wave, "This one's mine."

Both surfers race to deprive her of the wave. She smiles and lets it go, all along planning to clear the field and take the next wave, a solid five-footer.

She paddles as the wave rolls in and sweeps her forward. She quickly gets on her feet and charges forward to gain as much speed as possible. She cuts back up the wave, but at a tighter angle than she attempted before.

Torey watches as Cassandra catches air. This time she reaches down to grab the rail of her board and twists. His eyes go wide as she attempts a three-sixty.

She completes almost three-twenty degrees before she yells, "Oh crap!"

Wipe out.

Cassandra comes to the realization that she no longer fits in just one clique. She is half goth and half surfer chick. She is equally comfortable in both worlds. *I have spent the past five years dressing like a supernatural being, and now, all it takes is surfing to make me feel like a supernatural being.*

But it's not that simple. She has always loved the ocean. She loves the feel of the sand on her bare feet, and she actually likes the laid-back demeanor of surfer boys. She is shocked to realize that she gave up the sea so easily when she was younger, and only to protect her precious make up and appearance. But she will scream if she lets herself dwell on her past absurdity. *What was wrong with me?*

"I would stay in the water all night if I could," she tells herself out loud.

Torey paddles up. "That's okay by me, but I do have to wake up early for the competition tomorrow."

Cassandra grins at him, knowing in her heart that he is serious about staying out here all night with her.

She cannot believe that she just thought the word "love!"

"I want to be there with you when you sign in."

He holds her hand. "That's good, because I have a feeling that I am going to be a bundle of nerves. I am going to be sharing waves with some of the biggest names in surfing. What if I "drop in" on someone like Kelly Slater by mistake? What if I end up looking like a kook?"

Cassandra gives his hand a tender squeeze and grins. "I do not go out with kooks. So do us both a favor and do not "drop in" on

Kelly-freaking-Slater.

After sharing a good laugh about it, they hold hands and quietly float on their boards to watch the sunset before calling it a night. Tomorrow is going to be a big day.

## Chapter 11

# *What A Wannabe*

Traffic snarls the Pacific Coast Highway. Cassandra is anxious to meet up with Torey and get him signed in, but she and her mom are stuck in gridlock.

"Uh, I can see the Huntington Beach pier from here. Thanks for the ride, but I think it will be faster if I get out and jog."

"Honey, it's still a mile away," her mom tells her.

"That's okay, I'll call you later," she replies as she opens the car door.

"Bring some lotion," her mom tosses her a bottle of 30 SPF.

She can't help but feel both impressed and proud that her dark princess is actually jogging through traffic to meet her man. Though she still wears a dark ankle-length dress, at least Cassandra has the sense to wear a light blouse tied off at the waist. It's still black, but this time last week Mrs. Covent was resigned to having a ghostly pale daughter who despised the sun and spent her days like a troll under shady piers and overpasses. She doesn't know a lot about this Torey kid, but she likes the influence he is having on her baby girl.

* * *

Cassandra slows to a walk as she enters the staging area. She immediately spots the check-in area but doesn't see Torey anywhere. *Did he already sign in? Did I get here too late? Did I miss him?*

"Stupid traffic," she complains to no one in particular. She looks towards the surf to see if maybe he is out there catching practice waves. Torey sneaks up behind her.

"Sorry I'm late," he apologizes.

Cassandra spins around. "Torey! When did you get here?"

"My dad just dropped me off, but I should have walked, I would have gotten here sooner."

She kisses him. "Let's hurry up and get you signed in already."

She escorts him to the check-in table behind the last two registrants.

Torey takes a moment to scan the surf. "Check out the sets. Do you see how every fifth wave is a little higher and has a more powerful swell?"

The next surfer in line turns and says, "Thanks, I wouldn't have noticed that."

"Shh you're giving away all your secrets," Cassandra whispers to Torey.

"It's no secret," Torey tells her. "All surfers know how to read the sets."

She looks at the expression on the other surfer's face and thinks that maybe that is not entirely true. The dude before Torey finishes signing in and walks off with his number.

"Good luck," Torey calls after him.

Torey steps up and announces to the attendant at the table, "I'm Torey Kilroy."

The attendant scans the roster. "You're not on the list."

Torey digs a receipt from his hip pocket and hands it to him. The attendant takes it, looks it over, then tells the woman next to him, "This kid is not on the roster, but he brought a receipt."

The woman attendant checks the name and then checks a different list. "Torey, huh. It looks like they entered you in one of the female heats. I suppose you have your parents to thank for that."

The two attendants snicker at the lame joke.

Cassandra cannot believe that these morons are being so rude. "Fix it," she tells the woman.

"You brought your agent," the male attendant says. "That will cost extra."

He shares another laugh with his co-worker. They stop once they notice Cassandra's icy stare.

"Okay, we will add you to the male amateur heat."

"Pro-Am," Torey corrects him.

Both attendants give Torey the once over. "Kid, look, the pros are all wearing wetsuits today and they left their practice boards at home."

Torey is flustered, close to saying something totally uncool. Cassandra, on the other hand, is well practiced at dealing with miscreants like this. She calmly asks, "Is he violating a written dress code or equipment requirement?"

"Um," the woman says defensively, "he needs something to pin his number on."

"And just how do you deal with this problem during the summer events?" Cassandra asks slowly.

"I'll find a grease pencil," the male attendant tells his co-worker. He disappears into the crowd.

"Hop to it," Cassandra calls after him.

Torey attempts to lighten Cassandra's mood. "Maybe it's not too late to get you signed into the competition."

Cassandra cracks a smile. "Maybe next time. This one is all about you."

The woman behind the desk snorts back a laugh at the thought of a goth girl trying to surf. "It looks like you may have to go in cold. Practice runs will be closed in ten minutes."

Cassandra loses her smile. "I am so sorry that you were distracted by these dumb-asses before the competition." She digs into her small purse.

"I'm sitting right here," the woman says.

Cassandra snaps at her. "Well that is convenient. What is his number?"

The woman points to the number written next to Torey's name on the registration sheet: 67.

Cassandra tells Torey. "Lift your shirt."

He takes his tee-shirt completely off. Cassandra pulls a tube of black lipstick from her hip pocket and writes 67 on his chest. She takes his shirt and kisses him.

"I will be up on the pier. You go and get your practice run."

Torey kisses her once more for luck, kicks off his flip-flops, and jogs through the crowded beach to get into the water and catch a wave.

\* \* \*

The Huntington Beach Pier runs a total length of 1,853 feet from the shoreline and into the Pacific Ocean. It features a variety of shops and a restaurant that is popular amongst surfers and tourists. Today it is packed with countless surf fans all trying to find a spot with a good view.

Cassandra is still irritated about the rude reception that Torey got at his first surf competition, but she will be damned if he does not get to see her watching from the front rail on the pier. She squeezes in at a prime spot near a local reporter and a cameraman. She figures that out of everyone here, they would select the best vantage point and she is right. From where she stands, she is twenty-eight feet above the surfers and has a bird's eye view of the action. She will get to see the surfers catch their waves. They will pass by her at a point, where they would be most likely to perform aerials and continue on.

Just as Cassandra thinks that she can finally relax for a moment, Byron crowds his way into her already tight space. He announces himself by saying, "Oh dark angel, it breaks my heart to see you consorting with the living."

He spent all night coming up with that line and he is confident that it will win her over and back to hang with the goths underneath the pier. His pompous grin is full of promise and arrogance.

Cassandra loves Byron like a brother, but she does not want to deal with him today. She looks at him with a deadpan stare. "Why are you being such a chooch?"

Byron is taken aback. "Chooch? What's a chooch? Is that some ridiculous surfer lingo?"

"Look Byron, I am working things out," she says, tapping her head for emphasis. "I really enjoy being in the water more than I like hanging out in the shadows and I am really happy right now.

And this day is not about you. Okay?"

As the smug expression on Byron's face collapses, she adds, "It's not like we aren't friends, it's just that I am experiencing a part of life that I have previously shut out. I just need some space in order to sort it all out. It's all cool."

Byron's jaw drops. "You think you can fit in with these freaks?" he asks, pointing to the surfers and beach-goers. "Do you even know what they are calling you behind your back? They call you a Sheila, and a Cavefish Shea, and worse."

"I am not concerned with fitting in. I am just working on sticking my aerials."

Byron blurts out the only thing he can think to say. "Have it your way then. I am going back to school to watch the football game. Hah!"

He turns and storms through the crowd; or rather, he takes baby steps and tries to squirm his way against the current of people, but he imagines that he is storming.

*"Football?"* Cassandra wonders. She watches after Byron until he finally disappears into the crowd.

Just then, two goths that she has never seen before argue and push at each other and squeeze into the space that Byron just vacated. They wear thick white grease paint that is more clown-like then gothic. As they argue over whether this is a good spot, Cassandra comes to a sudden realization. *No freaking way! It's The Appalling Twins!*

"Hey it's Vampira," Sidney says. Evidently the goth makeup has given him the courage to talk to girls.

Cassandra smiles and plays along. "Well look at you two strapping young devils."

They each smile, standing straighter and pretending to adjust their nonexistent neckties. The twins are not known for exhibiting clownish behavior, but they are good at it. Maybe the makeup gives them the confidence to let a different side of their personalities emerge. Simon pulls at his brother's arm.

"Look, twin girls. Let's go talk to them."

They mock bow to Cassandra and chase after them. Poor twin girls.

Cassandra is amazed by the change in the twins' demeanor and recalls the similar change in her own personality when she first went out in public as a goth.

The cameraman interrupts her recollections. "So you, uh, you're into surfing?"

"Is that so hard to believe?" Cassandra answers.

"Maybe I can get some shots of you someday surfing in the sunset," the cameraman says. "It would be awesome footage."

Cassandra appreciates the compliment. "Sure, as long as you don't mind my boyfriend being there."

"Is he a Goth too?" he asks hopefully. "Is it one of those big boys over there?" He gestures in the direction of the Appalling Twins.

She rolls her eyes and looks past him over the railing. "There he is now. Check him out."

"Who, the grom without a wetsuit?" he asks.

"Yeah, the grom without the wetsuit," she repeats with irritated tones. "Just pay attention."

They watch as Torey and another surfer position themselves to claim the same wave. The wave is larger and faster than the rest because it is the fifth wave of the set. Torey takes it. He runs a good line to the bottom of the wave then cuts back up and catches big air, more than is expected on a practice run. Nothing too fancy and he sticks the landing. He is rewarded with cheers from onlookers on the pier and the beach. Cassandra smiles because she can see that Torey is not nervous.

The cameraman asks the reporter, "Is he on our list?"

"No. I don't even know who he is."

Cassandra butts in to inform them, "His name is Torey Kilroy. He is a local surfer and this is his first competition."

"He is now on our list." The reporter practices a possible headline out loud, "Local Wannabe Takes on the Big Boys of Surf."

Cassandra frowns. "It needs work."

Cassandra is aware that Torey stands out from the rest of the surfers by not wearing a wetsuit, for not having a brand new board, and for being different.

Luckily for Torey, Cassandra likes different.

\* \* \*

Torey is having the time of his life. He has been reading surf magazines since the third grade and recognizes some of the faces in the competition. He is thrilled to be out here with them, but he does not realize that he broke an unspoken rule of surfing by "hot-dogging it" during warm-ups. Some of his competitors have already written him off as being an "attention whore" and a "wannabe" and give him the cold shoulder.

The fact is, some surfers can be superstitious and are afraid to waste a good ride when it does not count, as if there are only a limited amount of good rides. Torey has always surfed the best he can on every wave he has ever surfed and he probably always will. He doesn't even notice the cold shoulders that he is receiving.

An air horn blows to let the surfers know that the competition is about to begin. All surfers except for those in the first heat must now vacate the water. Torey spots Dillon and paddles up beside him. "Hey Dillon! Awesome conditions today."

Dillon glances sideways at him. "Most surfers save their best moves for the scoring rounds."

Torey is surprised by Dillon's chilly attitude, but he is also amused that Dillon thinks that was his best move. All he can think of to respond to Dillon is, "Good luck."

He surfs a small wave back to the beach and looks for a quiet spot to sit as he waits for his heat.

There are sixty surfers in the competition. Only four will surf at a time. Torey is in the last heat, number fifteen. He looks around and sees that most of the other surfers have people looking after them, massaging them, handing them water bottles, and draping towels over their shoulders. Torey will have a long wait sitting on the sand without even a bottle of water to sip on.

\* \* \*

Back on the pier, Cassandra watches Torey sitting all alone, contrary to the other surfers in the competition who have pit crews, or possies, or whatever they call it. She struggles with the dilemma of giving up this primo spot to go and keep Torey company, or stay here to watch him and make sure that these reporters remember to cover him.

\* \* \*

Meanwhile, back at the Dick Dale High football field, Byron watches from the sidelines. He decided that he should watch one football game before telling the coach, "Thanks, but no thanks." As he watches the game, he notices that the Dick Dale Dolphins do not even need a punter against Mission Viejo. Despite the Mission Viejo Diablos having one of the best records in the last three decades of high school football, Dick Dale scored on every possession.

The Diablos' defenders were distracted and thrown off their game by the presence of a goth quarterback and receiver. The intimidation factor was working out so well that, during halftime, the coach had the cheerleaders paint up the faces of the rest of the team. The players even drew fangs on the dolphin logos on their helmets with felt markers. Claudia was even invited to join the cheerleaders. She had so much fun with it and did so well that she was made an official member of the cheerleading squad.

Byron suddenly feels both inspired and confident. *It would be sacrilege if I didn't join the world's first gothic football team.*

After the game he approached the coach and pledged, "I will do my best to make you proud." They shake hands on it.

* * *

Cassandra rechecks the pier. Unbelievably, it is even more crowded than when she last looked. And yet, everyone seems to be trying to get out of someone's way. She cranes her neck to see if maybe a celebrity is being escorted through the crowd. And then she spots him.

*No freaking way*, she thinks, *not now, it is too soon for this. I am so not ready.* Cassandra quickly turns away and leans her forearms against the handrail overlooking the competition.

The person heading towards her is considered to be a strange man by most kids in school. It is also rumored that he has strange powers. Byron has said more than once that he would give anything to have the arcane knowledge that this guy has, but Byron is full of crazy stories that he enjoys telling to freak out the newbie goths. Cassandra knew that she would meet him sooner than later, but hopes that it isn't now. A pair of large forearms rest on the railing next to hers.

"So you are Torey's girlfriend."

Cassandra stands straight, trying to pull herself together. "It's nice to meet you, Mr. Kilroy."

The Beachcomber takes her hand and shakes it gently. He waits patiently for her to introduce herself.

"Cassandra, Cassandra Covent."

He smiles and asks her, "Does my presence here make you nervous?"

Cassandra feels more confident, if just to spite him. She smiles back. "Well, you have to admit that you can be quite intimidating to people."

"I suppose that makes us two of a kind."

Cassandra gets his point immediately. She hadn't actually considered how Torey's parents might feel about him dating a goth.

She doesn't respond right away. She struggles to find the words.

Torey's dad saves her from having to. "Covent? You wouldn't happen to be related to a Millicent Covent?

"What?" *How does he know that? Did he run a background check on me, or something?*

She is suddenly suspicious. "I had a great grandmother named Millicent. What are you getting at?"

"I recall reading one of her books. Very informative."

Cassandra never met and doesn't know much about her great grandmother; except that she was burned alive for fear that she was a witch. She finds this whole subject matter to be draining.

Torey's father senses her unease. "My apologies. I didn't mean for our first meeting to be awkward. You were certainly a surprise to Torey's mom and me, but he is happy. Well, Torey is always happy, but you are good for him."

Mr. Kilroy points down to the beach where Torey sits leaning back with his hands in the sand. "He is growing so quickly into a man, and yet he is a good kid."

"He's a great guy," Cassandra agrees. "And don't take me the wrong way, but you and he seem very different."

"You are right about that," he says, not taking offense to her observation. "I mean, just look at him sitting there with his head in the clouds. I myself might be a bit more focused on the competition. Torey definitely takes after his mother."

There is a moment of silence, as neither of them knows what to say next.

"Cassandra," he says, "of all people, Torey's mom and I are not going to judge you by your appearance. We are not people that exactly fit in with the societal norms of this day and age."

Cassandra isn't quite sure what his point is, but it sounds like they are willing to accept her for who she is, and that's cool.

"Is Mrs. Kilroy here? I'd like to meet her."

The Beachcomber looks off into the distance. "Sadly, no. She is feeling under the weather today."

He returns his attention back to Cassandra and extends his hand. "It was a pleasure meeting you."

Cassandra shakes his hand. "It was very nice to meet you, Mr. Kilroy."

She watches him turn and disappear into the crowd the way he came. She is relieved that this meeting is past her, though she admits to herself that it could have been much worse.

She looks back to where Torey sits, waiting for his turn to get back into the water. He is still looking up at the clouds. She follows his line of sight and cannot imagine what he is looking at. If only she could see from Torey's point of view as a cloud begins to bear a stunning resemblance of her own face.

"What a day," she says out loud as she reflects on the rude jerks at sign-in, Byron's odd tantrum about football of all things, the Appalling Twins getting goth-ified, and now meeting Torey's strange beachcomber father. *Could this day get any stranger?*

\* \* \*

Torey shifts his focus from the cloud that he was willing into Cassandra's likeness and turns back to the competition. The commentator announces over the loudspeaker the results of the fourteenth heat before he calls the competitors for fifteen. "Smalls, Wisneski, Wade, and Kilroy are entering the surf for the final heat of Round One. Both Wade and Kilroy are local boys, and this is Kilroy's first competition. Let's give them a special round of applause."

This incites a raucous round of whistles and cheers from the onlookers on both the beach and the pier.

Not everyone notices as quickly as Torey does that the surf is suddenly turning choppy. The color of the water quickly changes from its normal bluish green to a muddy dark brown. Sand is being churned up into the water, making it grossly opaque. The ocean looks as if a storm is looming, yet the sky is still sunny with only a few puffy clouds.

Torey knows that Donovan is here, creating mischief. *I don't care what the conditions are, but I better damn well surf the same conditions as everyone else or I will throw this competition just for principle.*

He says under his breath, "You better keep this fair, do you hear me Donovan?"

Torey is now intensely focused on his competitors, if only to make sure that everything is fair and square.

The fifteenth heat gets the horn to enter the water for their twenty minutes. Torey's opponents are all experienced; all have had their pictures printed on the pages of surf magazines, but all three are visibly on edge. They don't like the looks of the surf, but they are here to compete, so they charge into the turbulent water and hope for the best.

Torey wades in and takes a moment to feel the movement of the water. He can sense its ebb and flow; he gets a fix on the patterns that it is following. He smiles because he knows exactly how the sets are going to come in. He has had this sense his entire life, so it is not cheating. It is a sense that all elite athletes possess. It is his X factor.

Waves that were previously rolling up to the shoreline now crash into it violently. There will definitely be beach erosion on this day.

Cassandra listens curiously as the reporter asks the cameraman, "Have you ever seen anything like this?"

He responds, "No. The water looks like a hurricane is approaching, but look at those wind catchers at the kite store."

The reporter turns to look. "They're not even spinning at all. There is hardly a breeze."

Cassandra butts into the conversation. "How is this going to affect the surfing?"

"That is hard to tell," the cameraman grins, "but it looks like I am going to get some wicked shots."

She looks to where Torey is paddling out. Not only does he seem calm, but he even turns and waves in her direction. Even from this far away she can tell that he is smiling and stoked to finally be in the water. She feels reassured and hopes that he sees her smiling and waving back at him.

Torey dives onto his board and uses long strokes to catch up with the others in his group, who are actually having trouble getting past the breakers. They are incessantly being driven backwards by wave after wave despite duck diving into them.

Torey offers them advice. "Duck in a second before you think it's right."

He takes the lead by executing a very deep duck dive that takes him under and through the wave. Usually you hardly even need to hold your breath to get through a wave, but these waves are strong and ugly, unlike anything these surfers were prepared for.

Torey breaks through and immediately checks out the incoming set of waves. He lets the first one pass as the other three surfers duck dive through it. He cheers them as they break surface.

The next wave is the fifth of the set. He calls out, "This one is mine."

His competition is not quite ready for it anyway, so they are more than happy to oblige. Torey paddles with strong strokes to catch it.

This is one wild wave and Torey plans to tame it. He speeds down its curl and cuts it back towards the rim. The announcer on the beach calls the play over the PA system.

"Torey Kilroy wastes no time and grabs a gnarly wave."

Torey already knows that he is going to attempt a tail slide, which means kicking the board around and sliding along the lip of the wave. He is almost at the rim and ready to kick out when the board pulls out from under him. He is shocked as he feels himself plummeting into a nasty wipe out. The wave crashes on him and pummels his body like he is in the "spin cycle" of a washing machine.

Torey is confused by what just happened but quickly catches

his bearings and prepares to swim back up to the surface. Suddenly Donovan's ghostly face appears before him. Torey yells in his mind, "You did that!"

Donovan smiles and thinks back at him with his mind speak, "Not me. That was Sirena."

Torey catches a glimpse of a mermaid darting through the sand-clouded water. "But why?"

"No time for questions, kiddo," Donovan says, "That wave was chump change. I am going to send out a monster wave. All of you will have a chance to take it, but it is up to you to make it yours."

The commentator on the beach announces that, "Kilroy has been down a long time. The jet skis are moving in just for precautions."

Cassandra counts to thirty-four Mississippi and Torey still hasn't surfaced.

*"C'mon baby,"* she prays as his surfboard bobs vacantly on the surface. Most everyone on the beach and pier quietly think their own versions of prayers and best wishes for Torey. Everything seems like it is moving in slow motion.

A large splash marks the surface as Torey bursts through. He quickly slides back onto his board and paddles confidently back to catch another wave. The crowd cheers as he waves off the jet skis and heads back to the line up.

"Kilroy is okay! the commentator announces. "And believe it or not, this newbie is paddling back to give it another try. This kid is definitely a local. Give it up for good ol' local California spirit!"

Cassandra lets out a sharp exhale of breath as the crowd applauds. She has new respect for Torey, though she thinks that he must be out of his mind. "Woo Torey!" she yells out.

\* \* \*

Neither Dillon nor the other surfers have caught a wave yet. They were waiting to see if Torey would resurface. They all ask him at once, "Dude, are you okay?" and "How rough was that wave, bro?"

"The waves are choppy, but the water is soft."

They don't exactly buy into his "soft" water comment, but Torey's relaxed manner is enough for them to consider taking a crack at the next wave. A relatively small one is coming, so Torey is going to let them have it. He figures that he has enough time to catch one more wave before the monster that Donovan promised will arrive.

\* \* \*

Under the surface and hidden by the stirred up sand, which he of course agitated, Donovan brings in wave after wild wave that the surfers are not used to riding. They are plagued with odd swirls and cross currents that are designed to keep the surfers off balance.

Donovan promised Torey that it would be a fair competition, but he never had any intention of keeping it fair. He is anxious to fulfill his part of the deal; he will make Torey cool beyond his wildest dreams and they can finally get around to bagging that nasty mermaid and free him from his prison once and for all.

Donovan's week off from hanging with Torey has not been good for him. He didn't realize it, but the kid has a strange calming affect on his mind. This week alone had afforded him too much time to think. His mental state has become agitated, though he tries his best to control his anger. If the world were "fair," he would not be in the hell that he finds himself in. His mind shifts into full-turmoil mode.

Wisneski makes a break to catch the next wave. It turns into a ten-foot wall of water that sweeps him up and curls early just as he is on top of it. He goes over-the-falls and plummets eight feet before hitting the water hard. One after the other, Torey's competitors wipe out on the sick waves and are washed unnaturally close to shore, far from the breaks and out of the way. They waste much time and energy trying to paddle back out to take advantage of more rides.

Dillon paddles up next to Torey and says breathlessly, "These waves are out of control."

"Pretty sick, right? And everyone is riding them wrong," Torey responds.

Dillon looks at Torey questioningly, "What do you mean?"

Torey points to the next one rolling in. "Look at this one. It is rolling towards our right, but look at the movement of the water on the wave itself. I would go left on this one."

Dillon thinks that he sees what Torey means and says excitedly, "It's breaking left! This one's mine."

He paddles out quickly to position himself to take it away from Torey, but Torey never even thought of taking this wave anyway. He was truly trying to help out Dillon.

Dillon doesn't really catch the wave as much as he is swept along with it, but he is on it and that is all that counts. He has trouble getting a feel for this weird reverse wave and decides to quickly switch to a goofy foot position.

The commentator tells the crowd, "Smart move by Dillon Wade by switching to goofy foot. This kid really knows how to read a wave."

This feels better to Dillon. He has never been on a wave quite like this, but decides to go for it. He carves a path up the face of the wave gaining speed and lines up for an aerial. He kicks out the back of his board with his right foot, expecting to catch air.

*Bam!*

His board jolts back abruptly as if it hit something. Dillon catches big air, but without his board. He is caught by complete surprise yet he manages to tuck into a cannonball position before he hits the water hard and plunges downward.

Dillon feels his body slam into a large fish. His mind races. *What the hell was that? Damn, that was a big fish — what is it doing in my wave?*

He can't see anything through the spray of bubbles from his splash. He spins his head in every direction trying to locate the fish, or shark, or whatever it was that slammed him.

One part of his mind assures him that it was probably a tuna. The other part of his mind just wants to get the hell away from here and worry about what it was later.

Dillon kicks for the surface following his surfboard leash back up to his board. He is almost there when he feels a hand grab his ankle and pull him back down. He yells with fright causing him to lose precious oxygen. Dillon panics and kicks his feet violently, able to break the hand's grip. He swims frantically for the surface with adrenaline-charged strokes and the last of his oxygen.

Sirena calmly kicks her tail and follows him up. Dillon's mind cannot register what is going on. He is too freaked out to think straight as he struggles against his reflex to breathe in and fill his lungs with water. Just two more strokes and he can breathe again. He is almost there. He is so close that he can almost taste the air. Just one more second and…

Hands grab him by his hips and pull him back down again.

Dillon knows now that he is going to drown. His body is spent. He struggles to see who his attacker is. Who could be messing with him out here?

Sirena pulls him down until she and Dillon are face to face. She embraces him and presses her flawless face right up against his.

Sheer panic drives Dillon to make one last effort to get away.

The gorgeous mermaid regards him with a somber expression, but her shimmery green eyes smile at him. Dillon's panicked mindset is swept away and replaced with intense feelings of unbridled love and passion. His body relaxes as he takes in the magnificence of the beauty before him. He suddenly feels like he is the luckiest man in the world.

Dillon's air is gone and he is fading fast. He can only see in tunnel vision, and the tunnel is getting narrower as water floods his lungs. His short life flashes before his eyes.

The mermaid presses her luscious pouty lips against his. All worries of dying flee his oxygen-starved brain. The mermaid kisses him deeply and more passionately. He tries to kiss her back, desperately wanting this last moment of his life to last forever.

His world goes black.

The commentator nervously announces, "Still no sign of Wade and he has been down for over two minutes."

# Chapter 12

# *Whaaat?*

Jet skis circle around Dillon's board and an EMT pulls on the leash that is still attached to the surfboard, which pulls up too quickly; it is not attached to Dillon. He holds it up as a signal for the scuba divers who are rapidly approaching by boat.

The rescuer looks back at Dillon's board just in time to see a pair of hands reach from the water and grab its rail. Miraculously, Dillon pulls himself up and collapses his arms and face on the board. He immediately passes into unconsciousness, but he breathes with shallow steady breaths.

The EMT yells out, "He's alright! He's alive!"

\* \* \*

Back underwater, Sirena swims over to Donovan. Of course he saw everything that transpired and that she kissed the surfer boy.

Donovan glares at her. He does not like surprises and doesn't grasp the implications of her actions.

She shrugs her shoulders for a reply and then rubs her rump gingerly where Dillon slammed into her.

Donovan thinks that the mermaid showed great restraint by not tearing the boy to shreds. Mermaids can be like that: as sweet as sunshine one moment, as vicious as a barracuda the next. It's their nature. He is forced to admit, at least to himself, that he understands less about mermaids than he thought he did. But he will have to worry about the ramifications of Sirena kissing a man underwater later. Right now he needs to focus his attention back to creating the perfect wave for Torey.

* * *

From her spot up on the pier, Cassandra watches as the EMT on the Jet Ski pumps his fist in the air to signal that Dillon is going to be fine. The entire crowd cheers with a communal sense of relief for the local surfer's well being.

Cassandra looks to Torey who sits alone on his board in the choppy surf. The other two surfers don't even bother to swim out to try to catch another wave. She begins to say a silent prayer for him, but is distracted by the cameraman who is breaking down his camera. "What are you doing?"

"There is no way that they are going to allow the competition to continue. Not after a near drowning. They will call it off any second with a blast of an air horn."

"Dude, would it kill you to wait a couple of minutes? Torey is still out there."

Cassandra looks to the judges' table. They appear to be frantically searching for something. She spots Mr. Kilroy stuffing something into his duffel bag as he fades back into the crowd. She smiles to herself and tells the cameraman, "I have a strong feeling that there will not be any blast from an air horn."

"Oh my God. Are you getting this?" the reporter exclaims.

Everyone on the pier is pointing excitedly at the wave that is now rolling in; the power that is driving it is awe-inspiring. It is a good three feet higher than any other wave seen today, and its overall mass makes it twice as wide as the others. This isn't just a bomb, it's a monster, it's a beast! This wave has muscles, and it's growing.

Torey senses the wave approaching before he turns to see it. He can feel its every ripple and surge. He has never experienced a wave even remotely close this one, and he knows that if he paddles ahead of it to catch it, it will overtake and crush him. He does the only reasonable thing he can think to do: he paddles straight for it with long, determined strokes.

"He is not going to catch this one," the cameraman says, "and it is going to be a forty-foot dive through it."

They watch as the wave sweeps up Torey, who continues to paddle up the face of it.

"I don't know what your boyfriend is thinking."

Cassandra has no ready response. She watches wide-eyed as Torey climbs the wave.

Many of the pro surfers who watch what is transpiring admit, at least to themselves, they would not want to be in the position that this kid is in. It is guaranteed that he is going to be wrecked. Torey and his board are vertical on the wave and almost at its peak, but it is already beginning to curl.

People on the pier are torn between rushing away for their own safety and staying put to watch this epic wipeout in the making.

Only Torey understands that he is exactly where he wants to be. He has fantasized about a scenario like this in his head dozens of times before falling asleep at night. He is psyched that he is actually getting to live out his dream. His timing needs to be perfect.

He rides up the face of the wave as far as he possibly can until he feels gravity start to pull him back down. He quickly hops up, plants his feet on his board, and kicks it one hundred and eighty degrees to surf down the face of the wave.

"Whaaat!"

Nobody is even considering leaving the pier now, or even the beach for that matter. No one has ever seen somebody catch a wave quite like Torey just did. Even the commentator is tongue-tied, and watches with gape-mouthed awe as Torey charges down and across the face of the wave.

"He…wait…what…not possible…"

Torey manages to keep his board steady despite the erratic forces of the water that struggle to tear it away from him, and the ever-crashing curl that is chasing him down. This alone will be enough to impress the judges and earn him high scores, but he isn't finished yet. He needs to gain enough speed to charge back up the face of the wave.

Back on the pier, the reporter is yelling, "Are you getting this? Are you getting this?"

The cameraman yells back, "Are you kidding me? This footage is going to be aired on every news channel across the world."

Cassandra hardly notices the press of bodies crushing her into the railing as the crowd tries to get the best possible view of Torey riding the monster wave.

Torey is totally in his element and enjoying every moment of this wild ride, but he is having a second thought about what he is about to attempt. A strange thought in his head is telling him to play it safe. He quickly drives that thought from his mind and carves the board up and down the wave to help him accelerate for what he needs to do.

The commentator finally finds his voice again. He calls the ride entirely in surfer slang, "Young Kilroy is charging this heavy kamikaze ride like da bomb. Let's hope that he doesn't hype out and catch an escort to the hack shack."

All eyes are on Torey, waiting to see how this ride will end. Even Dillon would be impressed, but he is currently being escorted to the hack shack to be checked out for his near drowning and inexplicable euphoric demeanor.

Torey knows that Donovan is not making this easy for him, but oddly enough, this knowledge allows him to relax and focus. He trims an incredibly quick line up the face of this impossibly ugly mutant, which is quickly becoming a double wave as faster moving water forces up against the back of it. The curl of the wave is going to meet Torey just as he reaches the spot of the pier where Cassandra is watching.

All of his senses focus on one thing: catching enough air to pull off a 360-barrel roll. Torey smashes through the curl of the wave and catches big air. A rooster tail of spray traces his line as he grabs the rail of his board with one hand and swings his other arm high and wide as he spins the board up and over himself so that his head is nearest to the wave and the surfboard fin is closer to the sky.

The cameraman is drop-jawed, yet follows the action and captures the best footage of his life. Through his zoom lens, it feels as if he is right next to Torey as he flies through the air. Torey completes his end over end and plants it with a tail slide atop the second peak of this double-peak wave.

*That was sick!*

He has never ridden a wave like this one and isn't sure how he is going to avoid going over the falls and being slammed onto the beach. He considers briefly that he might have to bail out on the backside and let the rest of the wave pass him by, but that is not his style. He cuts back down the wild chop of conflicting currents. The wave oddly loses much of its momentum and collapses in on itself. Torey easily rides the remainder of the wave back to the beach where he steps off into ankle deep water. Easy as crab cakes.

A swell of insane applause and cheering assault him from all sides. Photographers rush him to get a close up shot of the local boy who "took down" the Goliath wave. They are followed by a swarm of fellow surfers wanting to congratulate him for his gnarly ride, surf industry reps who think that he should be wearing their logo, new fans who want to share the moment, and bikini clad women of all ages trying to catch the eye of a young stud with a promising future.

In a heartbeat, Torey goes from being entirely in his comfort zone to being completely out of his league. He cannot take it all in. He cannot focus. He can only stare back like a deer in headlights with a weird, bemused smile on his face.

* * *

Donovan's head bobs on the surface as he watches Torey's moment of glory. He has kept his part of the bargain, and tomorrow Torey will keep his, but for now, he is actually proud of the kid. That wave was no joke. He was concerned that he over worked it, but it looks as if necessity forced Torey to seize his dynamism over water.

Three beautiful faces float above the surface to join his haggard face. They look at him wordlessly, but he knows what they are thinking.

"I know," he says. "Our work here is not done."

He knows full well that he has to keep the water conditions wild enough so that the competition will be cancelled for safety reasons. He pauses to watch Torey in all his glory, smiling before sinking back under.

Cassandra ducks and weaves her way through the crowd with elated determination. She is euphoric from watching Torey's performance, how graceful and powerful he looked in that amazing aerial. She desperately wants to be with him, but she can't get there fast enough. She can't get there at all. She is in the middle of a mass of people and can no longer even see the railing, let alone Torey.

"Excuse me," and "Please let me through," are having no effect. She feels claustrophobic and wishes she went with her first irrational instinct of jumping off the pier and into the water as a short cut. Frustration and panic start to overwhelm her. There are way too many people. She yells out, "Just get the hell out of my way!"

From behind her she hears loud booming voices, "One side, one side, coming through, coming through...." It's Sidney and Simon in their crazy goth costumes clearing a path. One of them grabs her hand as they pass. "C'mon Vampirella."

Cassandra can't help but laugh as they rush along. These guys are not the same Appalling Twins who bullied their way through high school. The way that they are clowning around is totally out of character for them, but pushing their way through the crowd is second nature.

Sidney resumes yelling, "Move it move it move it!" in order to clear the steps down to the beach. They rush down the steps two at a time and are faced with another crowd of people surrounding the blocked off entrance to the staging area where Torey is.

"We will cause a distraction and clear a path so you can slip by," Simon tells Cassandra.

"Lets do this," Sidney says. He squats down to let Simon climb up onto his shoulders. They do this maneuver like it isn't their first time.

Cassandra is impressed. "You guys sure are going to liven up the goth group."

"Nah," Sidney replies, "this goth crap ain't our style."

"Cowabunga," Simon yells as a way of letting his brother know to start moving already. Sidney takes a step forward and starts walking through the crowd towards the entrance.

People laugh and back away as the giant bloodsucker begins to sway backwards and forwards with dramatic exaggeration. Once the twins have everyone's attention, their swaying becomes more and more reckless and out of control. People scatter as Simon topples down, screaming like he is falling into the abyss.

Cassandra wastes no time and runs through the clearing and into the staging area from one commotion to another. She cannot see Torey, but she knows that he is at the center of the mob that she now faces. Even Torey's father is forced to stand on tippy-toes and crane his neck to try to catch a glimpse of his son.

Cassandra is totally amused by the chaos and wonders if Torey will ever get the chance to answer any one of the dozens of questions that are being hurled at him. She is really happy for Torey, and sincerely hopes that he is enjoying every moment of this, but somehow thinks he may be a little freaked out by all this attention.

Cassandra hurries over to Torey's dad. "I need to borrow your air horn."

The beachcomber tries to act all innocent. "What? I have no idea what you're talking about."

"Give it up, Mr. Kilroy."

He gives up the "Who, me?" act, reaches into his duffel bag

and hands over the air horn.

Cassandra snatches it from his grasp, holds it high and gives it a blast. The harsh shriek of the horn has its desired effect by shutting everybody up for a moment and catching Torey's attention.

"Cassandra!" Torey yells.

She pushes through the crowd and jumps into his arms, letting him swing her in his embrace. The cameras don't hesitate to snap shots of the surfer dude and his goth girlfriend. This is icing on the story. The questions are now hurled at them six at a time. Cassandra takes the lead and points to the reporters with the more relevant questions.

Cassandra overhears someone call her a "freakdudette." She has never heard that term before today, but she can grasp its meaning. She has been called much worse over the years, and this has become part of her identity. She has become rather thick-skinned, but somehow being called a "freakdudette" in this context has struck a nerve. She is aware of how she is looked upon by the surfing community. It is something that she thinks about late at night when she is trying to fall asleep. She struggles to determine whether it is her nature that makes her strive to be different or just old habits from when she was a shy, chubby twelve-year-old who did not know how to fit in with her fellow classmates.

Cassandra's attention is snapped back to the moment when a photographer calls out, "Can you get your Sheila to smile for a photo?"

A "Sheila" is what surfers call a rad girl when they want to get her attention. This is more to her liking.

Cassandra snaps out of it. She will not let herself spoil Torey's moment by being a distracted downer. She responds by flashing the brightest pinup-model smile that she can muster and hams it up as she poses for the cameras with Torey.

Torey has only one conscious thought: *This is epic!*

# Chapter 13

# *The Aftermath*

Monday morning arrives and all of Torey's memories of Saturday's events still compete for his mind's attention. He decided to walk to school for the opportunity to relive the events of his wild weekend in relative quiet. He recalls the awesome power of that wave and the adrenaline rush he felt as he was charging it. How he felt when he...

BEEP. BEEP. BEEP.

Car horns break his concentration. People point and yell and pump their fists to congratulate him for his bodacious performance at the surf competition.

Torey wouldn't know it because his family hasn't had a working television for more than a year, but the footage of his ride was covered hourly by all the news channels with headlines like, "Lord of the Waves," and "Torey Slays Goliath." By now, just about every surfer in the world has heard of Torey Kilroy.

Even non-surfers are awed and inspired by Torey and the wave that he rode.

Torey waves back sheepishly at every BEEP. His thoughts struggle to jump back to the reps from all the surf companies who expressed interest in endorsing him and promoting his surf career. One of them even gave him a cell phone so that they could contact him. It is now an unfamiliar lump in his pants pocket.

He finds it strange that people are pointing their own phones at him and taking pictures. Traffic on the Pacific Coast Highway jams up as drivers slow to catch a glimpse of the local hero. A bakery shop owner presses a fresh donut into his hand and congratulates him with a handshake as one of his employees snaps a picture of the exchange. The photo is destined to hang on the shop's wall framed next to the newspaper clipping of Torey riding the wave.

Torey picks up his pace and walks as quickly as he can to get away from the attention. *This is crazy*, he thinks, *who are all these people?* The last time he walked down this street he felt completely invisible. The feeling of invisibility used to really bother him, but now he cannot understand why he thought that way. He has never been so anxious to get to school.

Nearing the schoolyard has always put a knot in his stomach, but today he would be happy to feel that nasty little knot. If only he could be invisible long enough to sort all this out.

He is relieved when he finally sees the school building, but wonders why everybody is outside. His habitual thought process makes him assume there is a fire drill before homeroom. A sudden burst of cheering and screams let him know that this is no fire drill. Cassandra's mom's car has just pulled up and is rushed by a crowd of excited teens.

Cassandra was not as mentally unprepared as Torey for what is now happening. She knows how things can get when somebody gets as much airtime as she and Torey did and are now the hot topic on the morning news' shows. She kisses her mom's cheek and steps out into the throng to make the most of this moment.

Torey picks up his pace so that he can find out what is going on.

"There he is!" Some kid who he only knows by face points him out.

The cheers stop Torey dead in his tracks. Jocks, cheerleaders, mathletes, goths, and every other clique that has ever ignored him rush to congratulate Torey all at once.

A lump forms in Torey's throat and he is suddenly overwhelmed with emotion. He almost cannot accept that all these people are happy for him and want to be next to him. He often fantasized of fitting in by just having some friends to eat lunch with; this is way beyond anything that his imagination could have ever have dreamed of.

Everyone is shouting all at once; "That was sick," and "Way to represent, Torey," and "I thought for sure you were gonna die, dude," and "You are like our class' first celebrity," and "You are too cool."

The phrase, "You are too cool," resonates in Torey's head. He thinks that Donovan really did keep his end of the bargain. *He really did make me cool.*

Cassandra finally forces her way through the throng, yelling good-naturedly, "Hey, leave some for me."

She jumps onto Torey and holds on by wrapping her legs around his waist. She throws a fist in the air and belts out an exhilarating, "Wooooo!" The crowd responds with a resounding cheer.

Torey laughs like he never laughed before as he spins her around. His lifelong debilitating shyness finally crumbles and allows his long-buried happy and laid-back personality to shine through with full force. Torey makes the most of it and enthusiastically accepts and returns every fist bump and high five that he is offered. He acts almost as comfortable in this situation as he did while he was taking on the monster wave.

His fellow students have already forgotten all about Torey The Nerd Wedgie Magnet. Peers who had previously shunned or bullied him, or simply didn't know that he existed, celebrate his sick ride and his resulting television stardom.

The teachers let the students enjoy the moment, but soon start at the outside of the crowd and peel off kids, sending them to class.

Homeroom is still abuzz with excitement, but quiets down as Mr. Nussman approaches Torey's desk. "I believe a fist bump may be in order Mr. Kilroy." He extends his fist, which Torey happily bumps.

Everyone in the room laughs and applauds the gesture, which forces Nussman to try to once again restore order. The room is finally quiet when a cell phone rings. Torey and everyone else look around to determine its source.

It is Cassandra who tells him, "I think it's your pants that are ringing."

Torey completely forgot about his new phone. He digs it out from his pocket. He reads the display and shows it to Cassandra. Her jaw drops and she motions him to hurry up and answer it. Torey tells Nussman apologetically, "I have to take this."

He answers the phone. "Hello?"

On any other day, Nussman would have sent someone to

detention for using a phone in class, but he is as curious as the students as to what could possibly be so important that it would make Cassandra's jaw drop.

Torey's one-word responses from his side of the conversation frustrate the class. Finally he asks, "Can I bring a date?" He flashes Cassandra a thumbs up.

"Okay cool," and hangs up.

Everyone waits for Torey to say something. Torey milks the moment for all that it is worth.

"That rep from Quiksilver invited us to go surfing with their team in Baja."

The class gasps a loud chorus of OMGs that quickly escalates into a commotion that spreads like a tsunami down the hallways of Dick Dale High. Word leapfrogs from classroom to classroom: "Torey Kilroy is getting sponsored!"

Torey cannot help but wonder if this is what Donovan had planned all along, or if this is all becoming much bigger than even Donovan could have imagined. He decides that either way, once school lets out, he will find a way to thank Donovan.

* * *

Torey is happy to be in the ocean and to get a break from all of the attention that he is receiving. He hasn't seen Donovan since the tournament, and he is eager to thank him. For once, he is happy that the surf is calm as he paddles out from the shore, using only one hand to stroke while awkwardly balancing a large white box in his other.

Donovan eagerly waits for Torey. He feels a strange pride in this kid. All his plan required was that he simply ride out the wave and not wipe out and he would be the hero of the day. He would have taken this approach if faced with a wave like that, but the way that Torey attacked the wave was mind-blowing.

And now it is Donovan's turn. His mind is keenly focused on how to capture the mermaid who betrayed him and banish her to the hell that he is in. He needs the kid's help and is frustrated that he still doesn't have a solid plan at this point. Donovan is distracted by what Torey is carrying.

The white box seems somehow familiar. It has the effect of brushing the cobwebs off long forgotten memories. He catches a brief whiff of something that he hasn't smelled in decades, an aroma that he had forgotten even existed. He is struck by a sudden recognition.

"Pizza!" He manipulates the current to help hurry Torey along.

Torey laughs at the sudden rush of the water and almost drops the box. His board floats up alongside Donovan. They both have so much to say, but they make do with a fist bump and a handclasp. Then Torey breaks out the pizza.

Donovan hungrily accepts a slice. "Kid, you have no idea."

He is about to bite into his first taste of pizza in decades but hesitates. "What's this?"

"It's pineapple," Torey tells him. "It's good."

Donovan eyes his slice suspiciously. "That's not how they make it in Brooklyn."

*Brooklyn,* Torey wonders, *since when is he from Brooklyn?*

"This is how we do it in California. Just try it."

Donovan takes a bite, then another. Once he gets the taste of pizza, there could have been candy corn on it for all he cares. It's pizza!

He wolfs down four consecutive slices, rushing down every

bite partly because it has been so long since he has actually eaten, and partly from fear that a damned tentacle could reach up at any second to deprive him of this rare pleasure.

Donovan listens intently as Torey recalls all of the attention he is getting, the television coverage, and the call from the rep from Quiksilver.

Donovan polishes off the last of his seventh slice of pineapple pizza. He rests a hand on his full belly contentedly and is finally ready to regain focus on his end of the bargain.

"So are you cool?"

Torey smiles. "I am cool."

They spend the next few minutes quietly letting the ocean's swells roll past them. Both are aware that Torey has a debt to pay and that pizza alone is not going to pay it off. Torey is the first to break the silence and to address the issue at hand.

"So how do we find your mermaid?"

Donovan appreciates that he did not have to be the one to bring up Torey's part of the agreement. He realizes that Torey is becoming more than just cool; Torey is becoming a man. He needs to work quickly before he comes to his senses and backs out on this deal.

"Okay, this is how it is," Donovan makes his pitch, "This mermaid has distinct features that will make her stand apart from the average human. Her face is chiseled with classically strong, beautiful features. She has flowing long locks of golden-hued hair. She has the gloriously full breasts of a hefty woman, yet she is as lithe and as slender as an athlete. Her very presence is enough to dumbfound any man."

Donovan studies Torey's reaction and adds, "You probably have already seen a woman like the one I am describing."

Torey thinks for a moment and replies, "You are describing most of the women in Southern California."

Donovan thinks he knows where Torey is coming from and says, "Try to set aside your adolescent mind for a moment and think this through. Is there not one woman in this town that stands apart from the rest, who... well, who sends your senses reeling and your conscious mind asking, 'What if'...?"

Torey responds with a blank stare.

"How can this be?" Donovan struggles to find a way to convey the obvious. "Okay, up until very recently all girls turned you into a stammering fool so it is safe to say that you have no point of reference, but do you understand anything of what I am trying to tell you?"

Torey is not getting what Donovan is trying to describe to him and he is feeling a little defensive. Sure, girls made him nervous. *Was I really a stammering fool?*

"Look, I don't know what you mean by hammered features..."

"Chiseled." Donovan corrects him. "Classically chiseled features."

Torey keeps talking. "...And like, most women have blonde hair whether it's natural or not..." he hesitates as he realizes that Cassandra tries to hide the fact that she has much lighter hair. He regards Donovan with a look of defensive suspicion.

Donovan is perceptive today. "Your sweetheart is not the mermaid. She would have turned the moment she contacted seawater."

Torey knew that and realizes that he is falling into old habits by behaving like a confidence-lacking nerd. He consciously pulls himself together and takes a deep breath before continuing the conversation.

"Okay, that all makes sense, but when you say she has glorious breasts, they all have glorious breasts. I mean really, dude, haven't you checked out the women on the beach?"

It is Donovan's turn to lose some confidence. He has been distracted by the task at hand. He would have known instinctively if his mermaid were so close. He never bothered focusing on the humans on the beach. He reiterates.

"I am saying glorious as in goddess-like. This is not something that every woman is endowed with."

Torey understands that Donovan's point of reference is decades old. "I can't believe that you haven't already noticed, but this is Southern California, the home of plastic surgery, the home of unnaturally perfect boobs, and unnaturally beautiful faces."

"Plastic surgery?" Donovan asks.

Torey continues. "Women in SoCal, and I guess other places too, pay doctors a lot of money to make them look perfect. To make them look like movie stars and fashion models, or goddesses even. Around here, it's the not-so-perfect women who stand out as unusual."

Donovan scans the beach to find such examples of plastic women. It takes only moments before he spots three with the profile that could pass for a mermaid in human form. "This is not good. This could take longer than I have time for."

Donovan is concerned that he was blind to the obvious for all this time, but he didn't sense her on the beach, so there was no reason to pay much attention. He scowls as he thinks frantically to come up with a Plan B that will speed up the time frame. He snaps his finger and points at Torey.

"We can use your newfound fame to entice women to the shoreline where you will wade into the water in order to keep a distance. Surely they will follow you in. A mermaid will be naturally intrigued by you and curious of your mastery over water. If she spots you, she will definitely be in the crowd of admirers. Her curiosity would prevent her from doing otherwise. But she will not dare to step into the water, lest it betray her and reveal her to the world for being the mermaid she really is. It will then just be a simple matter of getting the one hanging back on the sand into the water. You may have to get a little rough with her."

Donovan is feeling better about Plan B. "Once you get her into the water, I can take it from there and everyone is happy. She will return to her mermaid hell with others of her kind. The rest of the women will have an incredible tale of a real live mermaid to take home to the dinner table. I will once again be free to leave the water, and I will let the coolest kid in town show me what I have been missing for all these years."

Torey is not at all confident about Donovan's Plan B. He voices his concerns. "Just like that? You want me to push women into the water? That is not cool."

Donovan knows enough to back off a little. The kid can think for himself and that's good, sometimes. It would be so much less frustrating if Torey would just go along with him. He pulls Torey and his board closer to him. "I think that I can increase our odds for success."

He scratches on the surface of Torey's board's with the ragged fingernail of his index finger.

"Hey," Torey exclaims as curls of fiberglass twist off of his board.

Donovan ignores him and continues to draw what is quickly beginning to look like a face.

"We will assume for now that she still looks exactly the same as she did all those years ago when she betrayed me. In fact, I am quite certain that a mermaid would never give her glorious appearance over to the hands of a plastic doctor."

Donovan deftly sketches a detailed likeness of a beautiful woman with a heart-shaped face, almond-shaped eyes, lush pouty lips and long flowing locks of hair.

"You can use this as reference," he explains. Her hair was golden blonde when I last saw her. I think that the plan must be to look for a woman who is oddly avoiding contact with water. Unless she looks like this sketch, you will not be expected to sacrifice your coolness by getting her wet."

"This all sounds kind of sketchy."

"Look kid, I just want to do this right so that nobody gets hurt and I get my life back, at least what is left of it."

Torey feels a twang of guilt, just as Donovan had hoped. He intends to man-up and keep his end of the bargain, even though what he has to do feels creepy and goes totally against his nature. He assures Donovan, "I will do what I need to do to help get you out of your hell."

Donovan smiles broadly and claps Torey on the shoulder in a show of appreciation. He projects an outward appearance of confidence while he attempts to mask the lingering doubt that he might be wrong. He tries to banish the mental images of the faces of the very mermaids that he has been trapped with for these many decades. He cannot deal with the thought that his mermaid could possibly, unlikely as it may be, have had her face altered.

But Donovan will be the first to admit, if only to himself, that there is a great deal about mermaids that he does not know and he will be happy when he does not have to look at the likes of one ever again.

# Chapter 14

## *Fame and Misfortune*

Torey walks alone along the boulder-strewn shoreline towards Laguna Beach, just north of Dana Point. Laguna Beach is a one-time artist community that has evolved into a high-end realtors' dream. Upscale shops, restaurants, and art galleries fan out from the idyllic beach and up the slope of the canyon.

The boardwalk is full of ice cream-licking, soda-slurping idlers who want nothing more than to make the best of a glorious eighty-degree day. The volleyball and basketball courts are full to capacity and the beach is crowded with late-season sun worshippers. It is the perfect place for Torey to draw a crowd of potential mermaids.

Torey has no idea how this is all going to play out, but he is already feeling a terrible sense of guilt, both for what he is about to do, and for not telling Cassandra where he is and what he is up to. He knows that he is indebted to Donovan, and he will do his best to pay it off, but he really can't wait for this all to be over.

The main beach of Laguna is just around the next bend. He passes by a restaurant with an outside deck full of diners, but it is high enough up the cliff face that no one would get a good enough look to recognize him.

He uses his remaining time to ponder the events of the past few weeks with his strange mentor and considers that he does not really know a lot about him. Sometimes Donovan is so cool and is like, well, like a friend. But other times he is really menacing, completely out of his mind and dangerously reckless. He is a real life Jekyll and Hyde. So which Donovan will show up today? He is afraid that he already knows which one is waiting under the water for Torey to lure the mermaid to him.

*What if Donovan is really a crazy stalker? And what if this mermaid is hiding from him for good reason?* And, *What if,* Torey thinks, *I am about to do something horrible?*

He is quickly getting cold feet and losing his nerve. He feels a rush of panic and a sick feeling that he is in way over his head. *I shouldn't be here.*

He stops walking. It feels wrong. His instincts want him to turn his back to Laguna and ditch this ridiculous plan.

A girl screams.

Torey snaps from his mental tug of war in time to see three girls rushing towards him. He has been spotted. All three are screaming excitedly. Heads turn to see what is going on. Someone yells out, "It's Torey Kilroy!"

Word of a Torey sighting has already spread to people at the edge of the boardwalk. People rush over to get a glimpse of the young hero.

Torey has no choice but to go ahead with Donovan's plan. He back peddles into ankle-deep water as a dozen girls crowd in to get his attention. There are already too many for him to focus. He is feeling overwhelmed and is forced to retreat further into the water. With both hands defensively in front of him, he attempts to respond to his fans:

"Hi."

"Hello."

"Thank you."

"Um, I already have a girlfriend."

"You want me to sign *what?*"

Two of the more aggressive girls have caught up with him and are having a tug of war with his arms, each trying to focus Torey's attention.

He is in waist deep water now, but he is in way over his head. "Ladies, please calm down."

He pulls away because it is obvious that neither of them is a mermaid and he shouldn't be wasting any more time on them. He can't help but notice that one of the girls grabbing his arm has really sharp nails. Blood wells up at the scratch on his bicep.

"This is bananas," he says with a shrill sense of panic. He does not want to hurt the two women that are on his arms, but he soon won't have a choice as a dozen more girls wade into the surf to meet him.

Donovan considers rolling in a rogue wave to sweep away Torey's non-mermaid admirers, but he cannot afford to tip off the mermaid to his presence. She would instantly sense his dynamism. He mind-speaks, "You are on your own kid."

Torey uses his own dynamism to loosen the sand beneath the feet of the two aggressive women that have his arms. They squeal as they lose their footing and their grip on Torey's arms, splashing face down into the surf. Donovan's voice enters his head and interrupts his thoughts: "She is here! I can smell her!"

Torey massages his arms instinctively to prevent bruising. He looks at the dozen or so women who are at least partially in the water and therefore definitely not mermaids.

Torey thinks back to Donovan, "Are you sure? These all still have legs."

"On the beach! Are there any still on the beach?"

Torey notices a young woman who remains about ten yards from the shoreline sporting a white strapless bathing suit. She is beautiful! Her green almond-shaped eyes light up her heart-shaped face that is framed by locks of flowing blonde hair that glisten in the sunlight. The shimmery one-piece suit that she wears form fits the lithe curves and contours of her perfect body. A shear sarong is tied at her hips.

Torey drops his jaw involuntarily; she is that beautiful. She smiles back demurely and invites him over with a subtle tilt of her head. He tells Donovan, "She wants me to go over to her."

Donovan's anxious voice blasts in his head, "Go to her, but do not step entirely out of the water. If you step out of the water, I will not be able to communicate with you and she could entrap you on land as easily as she entrapped me in the sea!"

"Wait, what?" Torey never considers that he might be in danger. He replies, "Um?" But despite his sudden misgivings about the situation, Torey walks towards her. *What does he mean when he says 'entrapped?'*

The blonde-haired beauty appears to be about eighteen, though Torey considers that she may possibly be a few hundred years old. It kind of freaks him out, but he steadies his resolve.

He just hopes that he doesn't end up being "entrapped" out of the water.

Torey stops walking toward her once he reaches the shoreline. He smiles the best he can under the circumstances and says simply, "Hi, I'm Torey."

"It is very nice to meet you, Torey. My name is Lyris," she replies with a smile that makes his heart skip a beat.

Donovan never told him the mermaid's name, but Torey reckons that Lyris would definitely be a perfectly suitable name for a mermaid. With a sense of relief he knows that he has not become enchanted by Lyris because he keeps worrying about what Cassandra would think if she saw what was going on right now. He forces himself to flush all of these thoughts from his head so that he can concentrate. He holds out his hands and gestures for her to come to him. Lyris shakes her head playfully and gestures for him to come to her.

Donovan is frustrated by his refracted view of what is unfolding. He can tell by the woman's gesturing that she wants Torey out of the water. He is alarmed to see Torey step toward her. The water is only up to his ankles at this point. He yells a thought into Torey's mind, "Do not step out of the water!"

Torey replies by thinking back, "Dude, I know. Now get out of my head so I can think."

He is distracted enough by Lyris. Her every move is compelling. She unties her wrap deftly with one hand and lets it float down to the sand. Her legs are athletically toned, perfectly tanned, and shimmery, but she does not use them to step into the water.

Donovan decides to chance raising his eyes above the waterline, but stays camouflaged by a clump of kelp. It would be very difficult to spot him and the harpoon that he clutches in his hand. *This is finally happening.*

He struggles against his urge to impale her where she stands, but she must be in the water and wounded. He must weaken her so he can drag her to the portal and send her back into hell. He feels only a slight twinge of guilt for not telling Torey that it is a necessity to seriously injure her. It would surely be impossible to drag a healthy mermaid three feet let alone as far as he needs to, and he cannot kill her outright because he must bring a living soul to the guardian of the hell in order to make the swap.

"You don't seem to like the water," Torey tells Lyris.

"I like the water just fine, but I cannot go in right now. Maybe a little later we can go for a nice swim in the sunset."

They are just ten feet from each other and are at an impasse. Neither is willing to take another step forward for their own reasons.

Torey pushes the issue. "It seems strange that you won't come into the water. You *are* wearing a bathing suit."

She counters, "It's not so strange because I have my reasons. But this is all rather silly, isn't it? If you would just come out of the water, we could be holding hands and getting to know each other."

Torey has no ready answer to her request. He freezes and has no idea what to do. He thinks to Donovan, "She might be your mermaid. She really won't step into the water. I don't know what to do."

"It must be her. Her scent is strong. You must use your dynamism to send a surge of water at her and get her wet."

"My dynamism over water sucks. There must be another way."

"Do not think that you can drag her into the water. She will be far too powerful."

"Why don't you send a wave to splash her?"

"She would sense my presence. I cannot take the chance and spook her. It is all on you. You must seduce her."

"Seduce her? This is *me*," he reminds Donovan. Torey does not have the lines or the moves to seduce anyone. And even if he did, he would not be able to lie effectively enough to pull it off. He knows that he is going to blow it.

"Do not blow this," Donovan yells in Torey's head.

Torey is shaken by Donovan's intensity, yet he forces himself to return his attention to the mermaid.

Lyris reaches down to pick up her sarong. Her stunning smile remains, but it now somehow seems sad. "This is all becoming rather awkward. Maybe our paths will cross another time, Torey Kilroy."

Torey knows that there will be no next time. He caves under the stress of the situation and steps out of the water to approach Lyris.

Donovan yells, "No no-" but their mental connection is now breached.

Torey panics and rushes Lyris in an attempt to sweep her up into his arms then rush her to the water. He is relieved that she is as light as she looks and that he is already ankle deep back in the water.

Lyris is shocked as Torey carries her into the surf. She shrieks with alarm as the water splashes against her legs. She quickly blots at the offending water with her sarong, trying to get it off of her skin, but it is too late. The color of her legs is already changing, turning lighter in blotchy patterns. She watches in horror as her legs change before her eyes.

Torey cannot believe what he is seeing. "You *are* a mermaid!"

He dumps her into the water.

Donovan yells in his head, "Now get out of the way so I can stick her!"

"What?" Torey is alarmed and repulsed by what Donovan just said. He shifts his position so that he is hopefully positioned between Lyris and Donovan's harpoon.

Lyris looks up at Torey, her face twisted with rage.

"What is wrong with you!" she screams out. She regains her footing and punches her two fists into his chest.

Torey can only stare with a slack-jawed expression. He retreats to deeper water in an attempt to escape her rage. She catches up with him.

"I thought you were...but you're really not...I am so sorry," he manages to squeak out.

She looks him dead in the eye and says, "You are not nice. You are just a mean jerk. A bully."

She slaps him sharply across his face. A tear runs from her eye and removes yet another streak from her newly sprayed-on shimmery tan lotion. A lotion that makes its wearer's skin appear shimmery and unearthly, but unfortunately takes twenty or thirty minutes to set.

Torey thinks, *I am not a bully. I'm just a loser.* He stammers, "I...I...I'm so sorry. I thought you were a... a...mermaid."

Lyris stares him down, her lip quivering. She abruptly turns her back to him and wades back out of the surf. The spattered fake-and-bake tan on her legs looks like an unfortunate skin condition. Torey can only watch helplessly as she hurries away across the beach and out of sight. Her forgotten sarong floats pitifully along the shore break.

Torey is mortified by his boorish behavior. He has never done anything to hurt anyone, let alone a sweet young girl who only wanted to meet a "cool" surfer boy. Torey is feeling anything but cool, and seeing that tear run down her cheek made him want to cry.

Peals of laughter from some of the women who initially approached him let him know just how uncool he must be. He hears one of them say, "He did, the dumbass really thought she was a mermaid?"

Torey's anger builds quickly until he is angrier than he has ever been in his life. No bully has ever made him this infuriated. And none of the many humiliations he has suffered in life have made him this angry. It isn't even the mocking laughter that now assaults him that infuriates him. He is angry with himself.

The girls and women who are laughing at him at this very moment are absolutely right. *I am a tool*, he thinks. He just wants to go home and be alone to deal with the guilt that he is feeling.

Donovan's voice enters his head and interrupts his self-loathing. "Don't worry, kid. It was too much to expect success on our first attempt."

Torey mentally screams back in his mind, "You were going to stab her? What is wrong with you, you crazy psychopath? I bet you think that was really funny." He thinks in a tone mocking Donovan's voice, "*She's here. I can feel her.* Give me a break."

Donovan is taken aback by Torey's rage. He softens his tone. "Look kid, I don't know what happened. This doesn't make sense to me."

"I'm done. I am not going to hurt anyone else. How can it be possible to find your mermaid if you can't even recognize her? And like you can smell her from underwater? I am so out of here. I need to think."

"Do not shut me out, boy. Just remember that you owe me. I made you cool..."

Torey cuts him off. "Cool! You think this is cool? You heard them. I am a little boy."

Donovan cuts back. "This is just a temporary setback. Besides, being cool one hundred percent of the time is simply unsustainable. You will be cool again soon enough."

"Unsustainable!" Torey does not want to hear it. He knows that Donovan is still talking in his head, but he is seriously distracted and can only perceive his words as annoying static.

He steps out of the water and onto the dry sand, effectively breaking all mental connection with Donovan. He realizes that he doesn't even care about being cool anymore. *What was I thinking?*

It occurs to him that maybe Donovan has been using him all along, that Donovan is really a creepy freaking nightmare. Obvious questions come to light. *What would have happened if Lyris actually grew a tail? And what would I have done if things went really bad and if Donovan actually harpooned her? I would go to jail and I would deserve it.*

Torey wonders why he didn't ask these questions a long time ago. He already walked fifty yards away from the unfortunate scene that he created and pauses to look back. He is surprised to see that the crowd of people has grown and that they are eagerly listening to the women recounting the event. People are pointing in his general direction. He hears a mixture of laughter and angry jeers.

Torey is nearly in a state of mental panic and knows is that he has to get out of here to think things through. He usually goes into the water to clear his mind, but that is not an option. He just wants to go home. He is not ready to face Donovan because he does not know what he would do if he did.

He grabs up a stone and throws it recklessly at the water, half hoping that it hits Donovan's stupid skull. Little does he know it came pretty close.

* * *

Donovan doesn't flinch as the stone and a trail of bubbles whizz past his face. He momentarily considers throwing his harpoon back as a response, but manages to control his temper. *I thought she was so close. How could I have been mistaken?* Her very essence was a strong presence.

A tentacle gently tugs on his ankle. It drags Donovan back down through the water and towards the damned portal. Donovan doesn't bother to resist. He is used to this treatment from his jailor. The suction cup grip has the odd affect of settling his scrambled thoughts. He tries to clear his mind so that he can focus.

His first thought is of the self-assured young lass on the beach with the poise and complexion of a goddess. *She was sensual enough to convince Torey that she must indeed be a mermaid.* He must admit though that the girl didn't look like Leona. *Her body maybe, but her face not so much.* But Leona's presence was felt.

*Surely Leona would not get her face changed by a plastic doctor.* But he did smell her. He sensed her even before the kid dragged the girl into the water.

*So where was Leona? All the women stepped into the water, didn't they?* Donovan tries to recall a mental picture of each of the women that were there. He doesn't waste time considering the screaming little girls who, even if they were mermaids, would have been too young to take human form.

He recounts the star-struck teens, all of which looked to be the right age, yet they were all in the water floundering around once they lost their footing. He double-checks his memory, *but no, they were all wet.*

And then there were the ridiculous older women. *Not a chance. Mermaids do not age.*

*But I smelled her. I smelled her essence. Leona was there,* he thinks, fighting back a wave of panic. He squeezes his head with both hands to help wring the answer from his brain.

*Was she in the water?*

*Can it be possible?* Donovan follows the line of reasoning. *Could she have been swimming around all along in mermaid form, watching my every move?* He considers that he would have noticed... have sensed... been even slightly aware if she was in the water. He was distracted, but was he really that distracted? Now it is time to panic.

*If she knows that I am here, she will definitely stay away from the water and I am done for. Or maybe she is confident enough to stay in the water to be sure to keep me in hell forever.* His escape that had looked so promising just moments ago now seems like a very long shot. *What will I do?* he thinks with despair.

Donovan drifts downward towards the hell from which he ultimately may never escape. The portal that he constructed is looking more and more shaky and unstable. A portal that he doesn't even understand how he knew how to create it, or why to create it. The only thing that he knows for sure is that his window of opportunity is quickly closing.

What he thought took only a few years to construct has actually taken him decades. He will surely lose his mind if he has to do it all over again knowing what he knows now. He is fully aware that he can barely keep it together as it is. He will become nothing more than a babbling lunatic if he has to endure this torment for any longer.

Panic and dismay assault his senses as he is pulled back through the portal. He begins to struggle in an effort to have a few more moments to think clearly while he still can. Once he is back in his hell, his thoughts will quickly decay and become incensed and chaotic. He grabs onto the portal's edge, but he feels it begin to pull apart.

Donovan is experiencing a total lapse of reason that rivals the first time that he woke up in this hell. This time it is not caused by the betrayal of the woman that he loved, but by the realization that he may never escape. He releases his grasp and accepts his fall into oblivion.

"She was there! I smelled her!" he screams out.

That is his last rational thought as he enters the pulsing intensity of his hell.

## Chapter 15

# *Cheer Up! The Worst Is Yet To Come*

The next morning, Torey walks to school and is thankful that his fifteen minutes of fame seems to be fading and that people seem to have lost interest in him. He is mentally numb from yesterday's debacle with the girl Lyris at the beach, and the long, sleepless night he had agonizing over what he could have done differently. On the one hand, he knows that he should go back on his word with Donovan, but on the other, he doesn't want to break a promise.

His mind is focusing on way too many things at once. Donovan's personality and temper are becoming more and more extreme. *What if Lyris was a mermaid? Would Donovan have really stabbed her with his harpoon, or worse? Does he really expect me to lure every pretty girl on the beach into the water? And how many until we find the right one? What did I get myself into and how do I get out of this? If I didn't know better, you would think that I made a deal with the devil.*

*What if I did make a deal with the devil?*

*Being cool is unsustainable? What the hell is that about?* Sure he was cool beyond all expectations for a little while, but ever since yesterday, all he can feel is the big "L" blazing on his forehead. Maybe yesterday was enough to make good on his agreement with Donovan.

Torey decides that he will give surfing a break today. He feels really bad about not seeing Cassandra yesterday and he really misses her. She will know how to help him sort things out. She's good at things like that.

Torey's spirits lift just from thinking about her, and he can almost feel the weight of the "L" lift a little bit from his forehead. He smiles for the first time since yesterday and picks up his pace. He is anxious to get to school and give Cassandra a big hug. She always makes him feel better, even if he can't tell her everything that he really wants to.

Despite his distracted state of mind, Torey can't help but notice that he is not being greeted by anyone. Instead, the waves and high-fives have been replaced by hushed whispers and muffled laughter.

Torey starts to feel self-conscious. He is getting a lot of attention, but not the good kind. This attention makes his skin crawl. This attention gives birth to an unfamiliar emotion: aggravation.

It makes him want to yell at all of these jerks. To tell them to get out of his face and demand that they tell him what is going on. To tell him why they are treating him this way. But he wont yell because he has an unsettling suspicion that he knows why they are acting so weird. He is afraid that they must certainly know about yesterday's beach debacle.

Torey is relieved to be at the school entrance. He can already see that Cassandra is waiting inside with the goths. She will make him feel better.

Cassandra spots him and rushes to meet him at the door. She doesn't say "hi honey", or even "hello." Instead she demands, "What did you do yesterday?"

Torey should have been prepared to answer her, but he isn't. He can only manage to stammer a lame, "Uh, what?"

"I had no idea where you were and now everyone is saying you attacked a girl. Is that true? What is going on with you?"

Torey is stunned by her intensity, and that she is making a scene. "No... that's not... it didn't happen like that."

She presses him. "What didn't happen? You didn't push her down into the water? You didn't make her cry? You didn't call her a mermaid?"

Byron decides that this is a good moment to put this meat -puppet punk in his place and at the same time impress Cassandra with his willingness to come to her defense. "Listen you little freak..." he pokes Torey's chest and presses his fang-blinged grill into Torey's face. "If you ever-"

If Torey was aggravated before, he is angry now, and Byron has given Torey something to focus on besides having to explain his actions in a crowded hallway. Without saying a word, he simply cuts off Byron's show of bravado by grabbing his cheeks, like an Old Italian grandma might do to a squirming grandson, forcing his mouth to pucker. Just as the bell for homeroom sounds, Torey reaches his thumb and forefinger into Byron's puckered mouth and deftly removes his prosthetic fangs.

Torey didn't have a plan as to what to do once he had possession of the slimy choppers. He presses them into the hand of a passing girl who immediately screams and drops the wet fangs onto the floor. Byron shrieks and scrambles to retrieve his thousand-dollar bridge. But as students hurry to get to class, the fangs get kicked further and further down the hall. Byron bobs and weaves through the crowd in a comedic attempt to recover his hapless canines.

Cassandra sees the hurt look on Torey's face and immediately realizes that she should have handled this differently. This should have been a private conversation. But she was freaked out by not seeing him after school yesterday and then having to deal with everyone assaulting her with weird accusations about her boyfriend. She definitely should have given Torey a chance to tell his side of the story. She wants to hug him, but....

Cassandra is shocked to see a cynical grin curl Torey's lips and hear the mean laughter that follows. She pushes both hands into his chest and yells at him, "You are not like this!"

Torey is snapped out of his unfamiliar enjoyment of someone else's misfortune by the look of distress on Cassandra's face and the tears welling up in her eyes. A streak of mascara and eyeliner runs down her cheek. She looks to Torey once more, her eyes pleading for understanding before she turns and runs away from him.

Torey is numb from the rush of emotions that he is feeling. Somehow he knows that he could only make it worse by going to class. He turns and heads back towards the front door.

"Class is that-a-way, Mr. Kilroy," a teacher reminds him.

"Back off dude."

He continues out the door. Torey might not realize it, but his once scrawny adolescent body has quickly developed into that of a man's. His latest growth spurt has filled in all the awkward edges with bulk and muscle tone. The teacher steps out of Torey's way.

His day's schedule is suddenly wide open and full of potential, except that he can't go to any of the places that he should be or wants to be: school, or home, or the ocean.

* * *

Cassandra sits at her desk in homeroom. She cannot believe that Torey is actually skipping class. She knows that he has never played hooky before. *What is going on with him?*

Her thoughts are interrupted by a peal of laughter. She looks up quickly and realizes that everyone is talking about her in hushed whispers.

"What?" she says in her best goth-ituded tone of voice she can muster. She knows by their reactions that she is sadly out of practice and is losing her edge. Not a week or two ago they all would have quickly turned away from her and pretended they weren't staring. But now, now they are still staring at her and even look amused.

"What?" she repeats.

The long pause is enough to make her more annoyed and suddenly self-conscious.

"You were kind of hard on him," one of her classmates says.

"What are you talking about?" Cassandra is uncomfortably defensive.

Like a dam break, the rest of the class chimes in with agreement and more comments like, "You tore into him in front of everybody," and "You like, blind-sided him," and "He looked like he was so happy to see you."

Cassandra can't believe what she is hearing. "I don't believe this. A few minutes ago, everyone was mad at him."

This encourages a flurry of responses.

"We were just going to get in his face and give him a *friendly* hard time over it."

"Who doesn't do something stupid once in a while?"

"It's not like he killed somebody."

Mr. Nussman shushes the class and takes attendance.

Cassandra has had enough. She rests her elbows on the desk and plops her head into her hands. Her natural blonde roots are becoming noticeable. She knows full well that she could have handled the situation so much better. She admits that she has no idea why Torey did what everyone is saying he did, or if he even did what everyone is saying that he did.

And people are actually sticking up for Torey. That is really weird. Up until now she was the only one who ever stood up for Torey. She imagines how devastated he must feel by her actions. It is not like her to be the dumbass. She is supposed to be the rock, the one with common sense and the ability to reason. But he really freaked her out.

Cassandra does not appreciate the sudden rush of guilt that she is currently feeling. She exhales loudly and decides that she will make things right and have the conversation with Torey that she should have had to begin with. She will get things back to normal, but she is going to do this her way and on her terms. Cassandra stands up from her desk.

"Excuse me," she tells Mr. Nussman and walks out of the classroom. To the surprise of the rest of the class, Mr. Nussman says nothing to prevent her from leaving.

\* \* \*

When Torey walked out the front door of the school building, he just walked and went where his angst-addled mind took him, a place he had only heard about, but had never been to: a clearing in the woods behind the school that has hosted class-ditching, hooky-playing juvenile delinquents for decades. To his relief, the place is empty today. He would rather not deal with anyone right now.

Torey sits down on an uncomfortable log. Oddly, it somehow helps to settle his mind. He is finally able to focus on Cassandra and how he upset her. He knows in his heart that she is more important to him than being cool. He even recognizes the fact that she does not really care if he is cool or not. His relationship with Cassandra will fall apart if he keeps hanging out with Donovan.

His mind reluctantly switches to Donovan. He has determined that Donovan is a bad influence and is pushing him down a dark path that he is not willing to travel. He did not promise that he would find the mermaid, only that he would help *try* to find her. Donovan does seem truly concerned for Torey at times, almost fatherly, but he knows that Donovan is dangerous, and that Donovan does not consider Torey's end of the bargain to be paid in full.

A rustling of leaves distracts Torey's attention from his dilemma. He glances up to see a brown rat scurry from the brambles and onto the dirt path. Torey jumps as it heads straight for him. Without conscious thought, his dynamism kicks into action. An eight-inch barrier of dirt rises to block the rat's path. The rat cuts right and Torey wills up another dirt wall. The rat tries to scurry around it, but Torey blocks it again with another wall. Torey has not been practicing, but his dynamism has quickly developed. Before long, he has the rat running frantically within a maze of dirt walls.

The poor rat is trapped in the middle of the maze and Torey just blocked its retreat. After some time, it seems to calm down once it realizes it no longer has any place to go.

Torey sympathizes with the trapped varmint's predicament

and feels that he knows exactly what the rat is going through. Looking back over the past few weeks, it dawns on him that he has been running through a maze, and it is Donovan who has been throwing up the walls.

Torey starts to feel sorry for himself, but before his private pity party can get into full swing, the rat does something totally unexpected: it leaps up then scrambles and smashes its way through the walls of its earthy prison. No points for style, but brutally effective. Once through the final wall, the rat scurries back into the brambles from whence it came.

Torey can't help but smile at the rodent's dash for freedom. *Maybe there is a way out of this.*

"If a stupid rat can escape a maze, then maybe I can too," he says out loud.

But what can he do? He can't simply tell Donovan to go away and leave him alone. He can just wait until Donovan is stuck back in his prison, but he would never know when that would be, or if he can even trust that Donovan was telling the truth about that. But he can come clean about everything and tell his father what he has gotten himself into. It won't be easy, but his old man, of all people, will know how to deal with Donovan.

"Torey-freaking-Kilroy is breaking out of the maze," he announces, though no one is there to hear it.

\* \* \*

It must be National Cut Day because Dillon, Sidney and Simon hang out across the field from the woods at a shady corner of the school building. They must have snuck out between homeroom and first period. Sidney is the first to spot Torey.

"There he is," he points.

Dillon seems relieved. "Okay, cool, I'll catch you later."

"Why do you want to hang with that douche wad?" Simon asks.

There is no way that Dillon is going to tell the twins that he needs to talk to Torey about mermaids. Dillon has not been able to think of anything but mermaids since the competition and his underwater kiss. He has a nagging feeling that Torey might know about mermaids, or that maybe his freaky surfer friend might.

A recurring remembrance of that kiss and a feeling of love that consumes his senses derail Dillon's train of thought. This has been happening to him quite a bit lately.

Sidney is impatient for an answer. "Dude!"

Dillon snaps out of it. "What?"

"Why you gonna hang with that dickhead?"

Dillon decides that it will be much easier if he just lies, "Did you ever see his mother? She's hot."

Dillon trots off to catch up with Torey, as the twins immediately fall back to their default mode of insulting each other. As if they share one brain they simultaneously call each other, "Dumbass." They both take offense and try to put each other into headlocks. Finally they push themselves away from each other.

"This sucks. Whatcha wanna do?" Simon asks.

Sidney answers, "I dunno. We could go see what the nerd's hot mother looks like."

They snicker and amble off in the direction that Dillon went.

\* \* \*

Torey is already halfway to the beach by the time Dillon catches up to him. "Hey Torey! Dude, wait up."

Torey stops and waits as Dillon trots up to him. Weeks

ago he would have been thrilled if someone like Dillon even acknowledged him, but now he is distracted by his own problems and doesn't want to deal with him right now.

"Hey, it's not like you to skip class."

Torey turns away from Dillon and continues walking without saying a word. Dillon is caught off guard, but follows after him anyway. He gets straight to the point. "What ever happened with that creepy Crypt Keeper-looking dude? Do you know how I can find him?"

Torey is startled by Dillon's question. *Why is he asking about Donovan?*

But Torey is amused by Dillon's description of Donovan. Somehow he had forgotten exactly how spooky Donovan really does look. After spending so much time with him, Torey must have gotten used to Donovan's creepy appearance.

"He's gone," Torey replies, and continues walking home. He still doesn't know how he is going to explain everything to his father, but he will just have to deal with it.

They walk silently until they reach the beach. Torey can't imagine why Dillon is still here. It's like he keeps trying to ask something, but can't work up the nerve to ask it, which is getting on Torey's nerves.

"Are you going to follow me all the way home?"

Dillon pounces on the opportunity. "Tell me what you know about mermaids."

Torey's eyes go wide in panic, but he manages to keep his cool. He tries to deflect the conversation. "Dude! Are you like, feeling okay?"

His mind races back to Dillon's wipe out. *He was under water for a freakishly long time. Could he have seen a mermaid?*

"You know, I thought that I was going out of my mind. I mean, it seemed so real, but with the medication that they gave me at the hospital, I almost talked myself out of it ever happening. They almost convinced me that the kiss only happened in my mind. Can you believe that?"

All Torey hears after the word 'kiss' is, blah blah blah blah. *Holy crap*, he thinks, *is Dillon telling me that he kissed a mermaid? Underwater?*

He is startled from his panic when Dillon punches his shoulder and says, "And then I saw her again the other day right there on the cover of your notebook. So I figure she is real and you know her and you can help me find her."

"Shut up," Torey tells him. "Just shut up for a minute."

Torey is not prepared to deal with this. He knows firsthand the effect a mermaid can have on a man's senses and he feels really bad for Dillon. Donovan once said that if you first kiss a mermaid on land you will live on land, but if the first kiss happens underwater you will be destined to live your life underwater. Dillon has no idea what he is in for.

"Dude, I'm not really sure, but you are like, totally screwed."

Dillon looks startled, "Why? What do you know about it?"

"I'm not an expert or anything, but I think you might have to live the rest of your life underwater."

Dillon laughs, "Don't be stupid. I just need to see her again. Then in a more somber tone of voice, he whispers, "I... I can't live without her."

Torey considers telling him to just paddle out into the ocean and wait for her, but he thinks he remembers Donovan saying that you can never be sure if they will be nice or if they will tear you to shreds. The only person that might be able help Dillon is Donovan. *That's just great.*

"Why did you go and kiss a stinking mermaid underwater?!"

"I didn't have a choice!"

"Just go home, dude. And stay away from the water."

He doesn't wait to hear Dillon's response, but picks up the pace as he is really anxious to get this done and behind him. This changes everything. He suddenly hopes that his parents aren't around to ask him stupid questions and give him a hard time.

Torey makes a break for it. He needs to get away from Dillon.

Dillon grabs at Torey in an attempt to stop him, but only manages to spill his books onto the sand. Torey lets his books fall and keeps running. The only thing on his mind is getting to his rack of surfboards and seeing if Donovan is in a mood to help Dillon.

There is no way that Dillon is going to just go home. He knows that Torey knows how to find his mermaid. And if he doesn't know, than maybe his weird beachcomber father might have some answers.

He scoops up Torey's abandoned books with the idea that he now has an excuse to go to Torey's house and maybe even go inside. As far as he knows, no one has ever been inside of Torey's creepy ramshackle beach house.

Dillon grabs up the last of the books, a notebook. He glances down at the drawing on the cover. It is a dead ringer of the face of his beloved mermaid. On the back cover Torey has sketched variations of mermaid tails.

He chases after Torey.

* * *

Torey slows to a trot to catch his breath as he enters his yard. He must be as stealthy as possible; he definitely doesn't want to deal with his parents now. Since he started going to school, he hasn't been home at this time of day and he doesn't know their daily routine. If his father catches him cutting school, he would probably make him do pushups and spar for the entire weekend as punishment. He expects to feel his father's huge hand grasp his shoulder at any moment, but he needs a surfboard, so he has to chance it.

Torey steadies his nerves as he sneaks up to the side of the house to grab his favorite board, then make a dash for the surf. He looks over his shoulder to make sure that his father isn't right behind him and sees Dillon quickly approaching.

"Sonofabitch..!" Dillon exclaims as he walks right into the brace of arrows that are sticking out from the Tiki pole. "Who leaves freaking arrows sticking out like this?"

Torey shushes Dillon until he finally shuts up. His parents for sure must have heard Dillon shooting off his big mouth. Torey freezes and listens. He strains his ears, but all is quiet. Luck is on his side today.

Torey silently creeps over to the board rack at the side of the house, but instead of grabbing a board and sprinting to the water like he planned, he hesitates. He hears something odd, a sound that is rarely heard in his home: he hears music. And not just any music, but rock and roll music. His parents do not play rock and roll music. In fact, the only thing that he has ever heard on the radio at home is when his father listens to the weather and tide reports on A.M. radio. Something really weird is going on. Do they always listen to music when he isn't there?

Torey's curiosity gets the best of him and he sneaks over to the screen door for a closer listen. It sounds like a song from way back in the seventies or sixties maybe. He steps inside because now he has to know what his parents are doing. He crosses the kitchen and stops abruptly at the entrance to the living room. His jaw drops. This is a side of his parents that he has never seen.

His mother and father are dancing like a couple of kids on a date and they are oblivious to his presence. His father is dressed in an ironed bowling shirt and khakis. His mother wears a light flowing dress that becomes sheer when she spins in front of the window. She moves with a sensual grace that makes Torey uncomfortable. The dance is seductive in a way that is not appropriate for anyone's parents, at least in the eyes of their child.

His mother rests her face on his father's shoulder, but her hands have no intention of resting! Torey quickly turns away and tiptoes back out before he sees anymore.

Dillon stares slack-jawed at Mrs. Kilroy. He has had crushes before, but this is different. If it weren't for his love for the mermaid, he knows that he would probably do or say something stupid to Torey's mother. He tries to recall if he has ever seen Torey's mom before. Did she ever come to a school event? Did she ever even just drop him off in front of school?

Torey backs quietly out of the room and knocks into Dillon causing him to drop the stack of books.

His mother pushes away from her husband and quickly smooths down her dress.

"Why aren't you in school?" his father barks at him.

Torey doesn't have an answer so he shouts back, "Since when do you listen to music?"

Dillon speaks for the first time as if announcing his presence, "I think that song was Redondo Beach by Patti Smith. My parents like that old stuff too."

Torey had somehow forgotten about Dillon and he cannot believe that he actually came into his home. His parents are going to be pissed. "Hey dumbass, who told you to come inside?"

Dillon doesn't answer because he is a too busy staring google-eyed at Torey's mom.

*Oh, he better not be perving on my mother!*

Torey waves his hand in front of Dillon's eyes to get him to stop giving his mom the creep-eye. He resorts to grabbing his shoulders and trying to forcibly turn him around.

Torey's parents exchange glances and his mom asks, "When did Torey become an Alpha?"

"I don't know," his father shakes his head and lies, despite his feeling of pride that he may have something to do with it. He keeps his mouth shut on that account and tries to change the subject. "It is not a good time for you to be here, Dillon. It is best you be on your way."

Dillon pushes away Torey's shoving hands. "I'm not going anywhere until someone here tells me what they know about mermaids!"

Three jaws drop agape. Torey cannot believe that Dillon actually said that in front of his parents. He regrets now that he didn't just grab his board and head straight for the water while he had the chance. He decides to play stupid.

"Mermaids?" he says in a mocking tone.

"Dillon, you're too old to still believe in mermaids." Mr. Kilroy notices the fresh scrape on Dillon's forehead. "Did you bang your head?"

"Honey, get him something sugary to drink. He's had too much sun," Mrs. Kilroy says in a concerned voice.

Dillon knows what they are doing and isn't buying any of it, "I saw a mermaid and I know that Torey has too. I'm not going anywhere until someone tells me how to find her."

Torey knows he has to stop this now before Dillon brings up Donovan. His parents are already looking at him with suspicious looks on their oddly guilty faces. He follows his mother's lead and says, "Dude, sit down. I'll get you some lemonade."

Dillon damn well did not come here for lemonade. "You spend all of your time floating in a flat ocean with that gnarly lunatic and you talk to me like *I'm* the crazy one?"

Now Torey's mother becomes really concerned and asks, "What gnarly lunatic?"

"I don't know what you're talking about dude," Torey says lamely.

Dillon has been holding his emotions in ever since the nurse at the hospital warned him to cool it about mermaids before the doctors pumped him full of some really serious medication. He had the sense to play along then, but he's not going to play dumb any longer.

"First of all, I know that wave that you rode was not natural, and I know that you have seen my mermaid, and-"

Torey cuts him off. "What are you talking about? Shut up."

"What does this lunatic look like? How long has he been bothering you?" his father demands.

Mrs. Kilroy is no longer just concerned. She is freaked out. "Honey, maybe you should stay out of the water for a while. You can find a new hobby like glee club, or street luging. Street luging looks like fun."

"Street luging?! Mom!"

Torey can't believe what she is saying. Street luging is dangerous, and no mother would ever encourage her son to try it.

He is feeling closed in on by his parents and Dillon. His newfound confidence and cool demeanor is quickly crumbling.

"You're all crazy," he yells. "Leave me alone."

Dillon picks up Torey's notebook from the floor and thrusts it in front of Torey's parents. "So what is this drawing on your notebook? Why are you drawing pictures of the same mermaid that kissed me?"

Mr. Kilroy gasps. "You kissed a mermaid?"

Mrs. Kilroy frantically demands, "Torey, what have you gotten yourself into?"

Torey feels a sense of vertigo. His chest feels tight and he has to force himself to suck in air to breathe. *And what is with all this sweat?* His thoughts are nonsensical and frantic. It's probably his fault that Dillon will have to live the rest of his life underwater. He let down Donovan who is going to be stuck in hell forever. There is no way his parents are going to understand any of this. He has a sudden need to get fresh air. And water. And out of here.

He pushes Dillon into his father and makes a mad dash for the kitchen door.

## Chapter 16

# *I Change, You Change, We All Change, And It's Strange*

For the past week, Cassandra has struggled mentally to make a change and she is no closer to making a decision. She wants to express her new surfer girl side, but at the same time stay true to her gothic fashion sense.

Cassandra finds herself at Roxanne's Designer Boutique. This is just the sort of place that she has always mocked. Roxanne, a mid-forties blonde bombshell, or rather a once-upon a time blonde bombshell, watches suspiciously from behind the register as Cassandra browses the merchandise. She cannot ever remember having a goth girl in her shop, before except for the time when a group of them wandered in to make fun of the tan patrons. Patrons that were about to spend enough to pay her rent for the month, but left without purchasing even a tube of lotion.

Cassandra is here to buy something more suited to surfing than her repurposed goth clothing. She pulls a frilly black one piece off a rack and holds it up. She thinks that it might be too obvious of a choice. She glances over her shoulder and sees the saleswoman return a deadpan expression.

Cassandra puts the black suit back and checks out a red one. She holds it up and checks herself in the mirror. *This could work,* she thinks, *maybe it is time to introduce a little color to my wardrobe.* She smiles, happy to have made a choice.

Roxanne, sensing that this goth girl might actually be looking to purchase something, takes the opportunity to speak. "A safe choice," she says, "but let me pick out something that would look just divine on you."

Cassandra frowns and wishes that the woman would just leave her alone. *Oh no, she is coming over and she is still talking.*

"Okay honey, why don't you tell me what you're looking for?"

Cassandra is not used to strangers having the nerve to talk to her like this. She has been driving them away for years with her gothic appearance and badass attitude. It is probably obvious that she is out of her element in this boutique, and that is making her appear vulnerable. She decides to back off with her signature attitude this time because she really does need help.

"I am, um, I am looking to try out something for, um, for surfing. I guess I am looking for a change in…" She is becoming frustrated and isn't really comfortable talking to this woman. "Look, I haven't really bought a bathing suit since the sixth grade. I don't think a two-piece is right for me, so…" she stammers.

"Say no more," Roxanne cuts her off. "I have just the thing for you."

She grabs her hand and leads her straight to a wall of two-piece suits.

Cassandra pulls back and insists, "Oh no, not a bikini."

"Oh please. Darling, if you want to look good surfing, you will definitely need a bikini. Let's drop this wishy-washy nonsense and be bold."

*If there is one thing that I am not, it's wishy-washy,* Cassandra thinks. *Maybe this clerk is right. Maybe I should just go for it and do it boldly. I might as well do it up and blow a few minds in the process.*

"Okay, I'll try it your way," she tells the woman, "Show me what you got."

Roxanne smiles and gives her the once over. She selects a teal green bikini.

"We need something to bring out those beautiful green eyes, and oh my, what is going on with those roots of yours?" as she peers at the top of Cassandra's head.

Cassandra is uncharacteristically embarrassed about her contrasting roots and says, "I know, I usually dye them myself, but I haven't had time lately."

"There is a hair salon right next door," Roxanne offers. "They are the best. I insist you pay them a visit when we are done. Better yet, I will call and see if they can fit you in."

Cassandra is taken aback by this woman's aggressiveness, but she reasons, *I am already here, so what the heck.*

"You're in luck," Roxanne calls out. "They had a cancellation, but you have to go right now. Come back when you are done and I will have some more selections for you to try on."

* * *

As Cassandra is seated in the stylist's chair, Sergio, the salon's top colorist, looks her over. "So tell me, what are we doing today, sweetie?"

"Lets just hide the roots for now," Cassandra tells him.

"Oh honey," Sergio replies, "this is sunny California. We need to lighten you up. Save that black hair for Halloween."

Cassandra is so outside her comfort zone. *I could always re-dye it at home if I don't like it.* She reluctantly agrees to go "a little bit" lighter.

"My natural color is dark brown," she lies.

Sergio checks her roots and disagrees, but smirks and plays along.

"Au natural then. Since you are a new customer, we will throw in a mani-pedi at half price. Your digits are looking raggedy."

*What the heck,* Cassandra decides, and relaxes back into the chair.

As the black chipped fingernail polish is being removed and replaced with a natural clear coat with French tips, the manicurist tells her, "I figured that a clear coat makes more sense for the surfer part of surfer girl."

Cassandra isn't entirely convinced by this logic and watches in horror when she next applies pink polish to her toenails. "Pink?

"That is for the girl part of surfer girl."

Cassandra laughs despite herself. *I guess I can wear closed toe shoes for a week and maybe Torey and I can have a good laugh about it later.*

Cassandra is ushered over to the sink where her hair is rinsed. With a towel wrapped around her hair, she returns to Sergio's chair for a blow out. He purposely keeps her back to the mirror as he dries her hair. After thirty minutes, he is finished.

"And now for the magic," Sergio announces as he slowly spins the chair and faces Cassandra towards the mirror.

Cassandra looks for her reflection in the mirror, but she doesn't see herself. All she sees is some blonde chick looking back at her. She watches with alarm as the jaw of the blonde girl staring back at her drops at the same time her jaw drops.

"What? No..." *This is a nightmare.*

"I agreed to go a little lighter, not full out blonde."

Cassandra doesn't recall that the word 'blonde' was ever mentioned in the conversation. She feels violated. Waves of anger, panic, and confusion wash over her. She sits paralyzed staring at this alternate-universe version of herself.

She feels nausiated and bolts out of the chair to the bathroom. She bends over the sink and splashes cold water onto her face. She straightens up and stares into the mirror and watches as lines of black mascara and eyeliner run down her cheeks.

"Oh, doesn't this just look great," she says as tears well up in her eyes. She takes a paper towel and wipes off her running eye makeup along with the rest of her pale goth makeup.

Cassandra now looks like a typical surfer girl off the cover of any surf magazine. She is suddenly the person that she has been hiding from for all these years. *I'm not different anymore.*

She tries out her signature glare that she uses to intimidate those who get in her face. She isn't sure that it will work. Cassandra pulls herself together and emerges from the bathroom looking refreshed, but not at all happy.

Sergio sees her and gushes. "Darling, it's like a dark cloud has been lifted and hello sunshine. Just look at you, you are absolutely stunning and you aren't even wearing makeup."

Cassandra desperately wants to get back to her comfort zone. "Maybe we should change it back."

Sergio intercepts this line of thought. "Oh honey, you look gorgeous. Besides another treatment today would be too damaging for your hair. If you are still not satisfied in two weeks, come back and I will return your hair to your favorite shade of black. Free of charge."

Lately, Cassandra had been wondering what it would be like to look like a surfer chick, but that was a passing fantasy, or was it? *This is all happening too quickly.*

At this point, she admits defeat. *Well, I am already so far down the rabbit hole.*

She does not have it in her to thank anyone for their efforts as she pays and leaves. She swings open the door and freezes on the sidewalk like a deer in the headlights. *This cannot be happening.*

Byron, of all people, is walking down the sidewalk and heading straight for her. His tongue is working at one of his fangs as if there is a scrap of food caught in it. *He must be worried about me and is looking for me,* she thinks.

She stares at him with a mortified expression, but to her relief and disappointment, Byron doesn't even recognize her. He just passes right by her and says, "Take a picture Barbie, it'll last longer."

*Barbie? How could he not recognize his best friend?* She wants to chase him down and get in his stupid face for calling her Barbie, of all things, but a creeping sense of doubt causes her to think better of it.

"What have I done?" she asks out loud to no one in particular. She wonders how everyone at school will treat her now that her dark façade has been stripped away. She tries to convince herself that she can still be goth with blonde hair. *I still have my fashion sense,* she thinks, *I will just have to find a way to pull it off.* Cassandra grimaces with the realization that she is dressed entirely in black and Byron couldn't see past the blonde hair.

Roxanne swings open the door of her boutique. She shrieks excitedly, "Cassie! Oh my God! I did not even recognize you. Aaahhhh!" She quickly settles back down to normal volume once she realizes that Cassandra is not shrieking along with her.

"It's Cassandra," she reminds her.

"Of course it is dear."

She takes Cassandra's hand and leads her back into the shop. "You are going to just love what I have selected for you."

Roxanne has a number of outfits laid out for Cassandra to try on: bikinis, beach wraps, sundresses, sun glasses, hats, hand bags and shoes, all of which are light and bright and cheery and feminine.

"Oh no," Cassandra protests, "I am not going there."

"Oh yes," Roxanne insists. "I took you for a shock and awe kind of girl, a lady who makes a bold statement, a woman who will settle for no less than to blow people's minds."

Roxanne can tell that this goth girl is still mentally fighting against her transformation. "So are you going to go all the way and freak out everyone in your world, or are you going to go against your nature and be a wimp?"

Cassandra's current frazzled state of mind is no match for Roxanne's reverse logic. She exhales deeply as she grapples with the enormity of the situation that she now finds herself in. She feels like she is on the back of a runaway train and up ahead the bridge is out.

\* \* \*

Torey bolts out of the kitchen door. His mother and father and Dillon are all yelling after him. He pauses long enough to block the door by dragging a wooden barrel filled with old buoys in front of it. He grabs his favorite shortboard and knocks over the entire quiver of boards in his rush. He does not have the time to deal with it and hauls ass towards the water.

He hears the kitchen door knocking into the barrel wildly as his father tries to clear the way. "Torey, you get back here right now!"

He thinks he faintly hears someone calling his name from way down the beach. He sees only a blonde girl and the Appalling Twins, but nothing fully registers as his mind is in complete panic mode.

Torey has officially lost his cool. *I am going to be in so much trouble. I gave Donovan my word, but we didn't find the mermaid. What if he becomes trapped in hell before I can make things right with him and figure out how to save stupid Dillon? Am I going to get suspended from school for cutting class? Cassandra would know how to fix this mess, but she is really mad at me. I will feel so much better once I get in the water.*

*  *  *

Mrs. Kilroy has a sinking feeling of what must be going on. "Could he really have been surfing with the demon all this time? How bad is this?"

The Beachcomber shakes his head. "I don't know. We might be jumping the gun on this."

He sees that something has caught his wife's eye and follows her gaze. She is looking at the picture of the mermaid that Donovan scratched into Torey's board with his fingernail. She recognizes the likeness.

"How did you let this happen?!" she screams at her husband.

"It is probably not as bad as it seems," he says defensively.

Mrs. Kilroy disagrees. She orders her husband, "Honey, move your ass!"

Her husband has already sprung into action and is dragging a tarp off a black fiberglass speedboat.

She doesn't wait for him. She rushes towards the beach, grabbing what she needs as she runs.

* * *

Cassandra yells down the beach to get Torey's attention. She is actually happy to see Torey with his surfboard. *He is going to freak out when he sees me,* she thinks.

She is coming to terms with her new look, if not actually embracing it. She has already passed the Appalling Twins on the beach and they had no clue as to who she was. They actually started pushing one another, each declaring, "I saw her first."

*I could have fun with this,* she laughs to herself, *but first things first.* She picks up her pace so she can be at the shoreline where Torey can spot her as he rides in on his first wave. *This is going to be so perfect.*

A monkey wrench hits Cassandra's plan when sees Dillon running behind Torey. *Oh no, why is he here? That dumbass is going to ruin everything.* She quickly realizes that Dillon isn't just running behind Torey, but that he is actually chasing after him. She starts to run towards whatever is going on, swearing to herself that she will hurt Dillon if he lays a hand on Torey. She isn't used to wearing open-toed sandals and stumbles a few times before she kicks them off.

The twins see that a fight is brewing between Dillon and Torey. Torey is due for a smack down, and they will do everything they can to instigate a fight.

Torey runs as fast as he can, but feels footsteps pounding the sand behind him and quickly gaining on him.

Dillon is running full speed and yelling, "Oh no you don't!"

"Oh yes I do," Torey says. He uses his dynamism over earth to loosen the sand underneath Dillon's next step and hears a satisfying "Oomph," as Dillon goes down.

Torey skims his board into the water and dives onto it. He is instantly relieved when the cool Pacific water splashes his nerve-wracked body. He doesn't look back as he paddles hurriedly for deeper waters. He is startled when Donovan surfaces before him not even twenty yards from the shore, and without even the cover of fog. He is in full view of everyone. A large tentacle raises a swell of water just beyond Donovan, but doesn't break the surface. Torey yells a warning, "It's right behind you!"

Donovan doesn't bother to look back. "Kid, calm down. You're all freaked out."

"But-"

"The beast is actually here to help me this time."

Torey looks out in all directions trying to understand the situation. The octopus' arms are agitated and thrashing just below the water's surface. Dillon is floundering in the sand up to his waist. Torey's mother is running towards the beach with a towel draped over her arm. She looks really pissed off and really freaked out. At the same time his father is struggling to drag a boat across the beach by a trailer hitch. None of this makes any sense.

"Kid," Donovan lightly slaps Torey's face to get his attention. "Be cool. I don't have much time left. We need to move fast."

Torey regains his focus, but is still more confused than ever. "What are we going to do? You're going to be stuck in hell and Dillon has to live underwater with a mermaid and I don't want to hurt any more girls."

"Torey, I was so sure that we had the mermaid the other day. She was there, but not in a way I could ever have imagined. Her essence was strong in the water, but it was not any of those silly bimbos that you attracted."

"Then where was she if she wasn't there?"

"One of those women scratched your arm," Donovan reminds him.

"What are you talking about? Who cares? I barely felt it."

"You are not going to want to believe what I am about to tell you. Holy—"

Donovan is cut off mid-sentence when he quickly rolls off his board and tilts it up in front of him as two crossbow bolts pierce the wood. Thwack. Thwack. A third bolt misses and sizzles into the water.

Torey shrieks and dives off his board and into the water. He looks shoreward to see who is attacking them. He cannot recall ever seeing his mother on the beach before, but there she is with a crossbow strapped to her forearm, lining up another shot.

His mom is scanning the waters for Donovan. "Just get back up on your surfboard, honey," she calls out.

Donovan's crusty old harpoon explodes from the water and flies straight at his mother. It arcs high and looks to be on target.

"Mom! Look out!"

Mrs. Kilroy deftly steps back as the harpoon buries itself deep into the sand just inches in front of her. Donovan's head resurfaces just behind Torey and he puts his hand on the top of Torey's head and grabs his hair. "What are ya gonna do now, Mommy?" he says menacingly.

"You keep your hands off him you son of a bastard," Torey's mother threatens. She continues to aim the crossbow, hoping for an open shot.

Donovan laughs. "I promise that this is not how I saw it playing out, but it just so happens that your mother has been keeping a little secret from you."

"What the hell are you talking about?" He struggles to break Donovan's grip, but he can't. Donovan easily presses Torey's head beneath the water. He glares at Torey's mother, daring her to just try and save her son. Then he disappears beneath the surface too.

On shore, Torey's mom looks back frantically as her husband struggles to drag the boat across the sand. She snaps at Dillon, "You! Help him with the boat!"

Dillon regains his footing and runs to help the old man.

The Beachcomber yells to his wife, "Go ahead! I'll catch up!"

He continues to struggle with the boat, yet pauses to watch as his wife dives into a wave. He never gets tired of watching what happens when his woman gets wet with salt water.

As Mrs. Kilroy runs into the water, it explodes and boils with a supernatural charge of incandescence. She doesn't take but three strides before her legs fuse together and change from pale peach tones to green and silver with black striations as she dives into a wave.

As she surfaces, her close-cropped brunette hair sprouts wildly into flowing locks of wavy corn silk-blonde hair. Scales form in a wave from her hips, miraculously fanning into a large fish tail. She flops about in the shallow water until swells of water rush around her as she wills the ocean to do her bidding. She kicks her powerful tail and breaks water twice like a dolphin before disappearing from sight.

"I knew it," Dillon shouts joyously, "I knew it." He asks the Beachcomber, "Are you a mermaid too?"

"Don't be a dumb ass," the Beachcomber responds. "Now help me with this damn boat!"

# Chapter 17

# *Hell Hath No Fury Like A Mermaid Scorned*

Cassandra stops dead in her tracks as she witnesses first the crossbow shooting and then the transformation. Torey was right. Mermaids do exist, but foremost in her state of mind is the thought that Torey needs help. She spots the twins back peddling away in terror. "Hey dumbasses, help them with that boat," she yells at them.

The twins don't move to help untilshe barks like a drill sergeant, "I said now! Move it!"

They obey the commands of the pushy blonde chick and rush to help. They get on either side of the boat and help push the trailer with its old wheels through the soft sand. The four of them manage to get the boat to the water pretty quickly. The Beachcomber undoes the tie and instructs everyone to give it one good heave to separate the boat from the trailer. He jumps aboard once it is in the water and fires up the engines.

Dillon doesn't wait for an invitation. He climbs aboard like he belongs there and says, "This is one serious ride."

The Beachcomber is not thrilled that Dillon is on board. "Black Ops," he tells Dillon, "I need you to climb aft and release the dip flush valve."

Dillon peers over the back of the boat. "I don't see any valves."

"It's at the waterline. We don't have time. Just hurry up and feel around for it."

Dillon stretches over and frantically runs his fingers along the waterline to find the dip flush valve.

Once Dillon is stretched to the max, the old man guns the engines hard. The small, but powerful Black Ops boat lurches forward. Dillon is caught by surprise as he sprawls overboard and belly flops into the water.

"Hey!"

Mr. Kilroy laughs heartily despite the gravity of the situation that his wife and son are in. He waves and calls out a thank you to the boys, but he is surprised to hear a chuckle and looks back.

Cassandra squats at the side of the boat right at his blind spot. "Don't even try that Dip Flush crap on me, Mr. Kilroy."

Dillon yells after the boat, "That was totally uncalled for, dude."

Simon yells to Dillon, "Get out of the water!"

Sidney adds, "There are monsters in there. A big fish just ate that dude's mother."

Dillon shakes his head, but isn't going to bother explaining it all to them. "Who was the blonde chick?"

Sidney answers, "I don't know, but..."

"...she was mean," Simon finishes the sentence.

"C'mon," Dillon says, "maybe there's another boat. We have

to follow them."

He runs back to the lean-to by Torey's house. The twins watch him sprint off into action, but decide to run away and get back to school where it's safe. They keep plenty of distance between themselves and the shoreline.

* * *

The Beachcomber has a decision to make. On the one hand, he knows that if he brings the girl she will be in grave danger and will surely be in the way; on the other hand, there is no time to waste. He knows that he should scoop her up and simply dump her in the drink, and...

Cassandra has her back to him and is rummaging through a stowage compartment. *Now is the time,* he thinks, but despite his better judgment he is actually quite impressed when she pulls out a large knife with a plastic holster and proceeds to strap it to her right thigh. She wasn't even alarmed, and she didn't do a double take at the array of weaponry and grenades that are stowed beside the knives. In fact, she is already testing the weight of one of the smaller pistols. She pops the magazine to see if it is loaded.

He convinces himself that she will be all right. "The ammo is stored under a floorboard."

Cassandra locates and opens a box of 9mms and proceeds to fill the magazine.

He pushes the throttle forward. The engine lets out a high pitch squeal for the effort. He reasons to himself that she is Torey's girlfriend and now is as good a time as any to let her find out what she's in for with this family. "So you're a blonde now."

Cassandra doesn't bother to glance up from her task at hand. She replies with an equally obvious statement. "So Torey is the son of a mermaid."

The Beachcomber has nothing to say at this point except, "Hold on. This is going to be one wild ride."

He pushes the throttle to the limit. The old military boat skims effortlessly across the ocean's surface.

\* \* \*

Octopi are much quicker than they look. The giant octopus is pulling Donovan and Torey quickly through the water and towards the portal. Torey is struggling frantically against being dragged downward toward a strange red glow at the ocean's floor. He has fought himself free from Donovan's grip, but he cannot break free from the octopus' sinewy tentacle. Donovan talks to Torey with his underwater mind speak.

"Chill out kid, we're almost there. I have a good feeling about this."

Torey has a bad gut feeling about this. In fact, he is pretty sure that the red glow that they are headed for is the hell that Donovan has been trapped in. None of this makes sense to Torey, or does it? *Did she never come down to the beach because of what would happen if she got wet? Did she not go to a doctor because they would find out she isn't human?* He drives these thoughts from his mind for now and decides to try to stay focused, in survival mode, because his mother is in danger. Yet he wonders how everything got so out of control.

*I just wanted to be cool.*

Donovan has provided him with a funnel of air, but Torey has no intention of relying on him. He conjures up his dynamism to draw down his own air funnel just to play it safe.

Torey tries his best to reason out the facts: *My mom was shooting arrows at Donovan. That is pretty messed up. Donovan thinks she is the mermaid who cursed him. That is* really *messed up. And what was that crazy explosion at the shoreline that sent twists of iridescent green light everywhere?* A cold shiver creeps up his spine with the sinking realization that his mother is the mermaid. *Does this mean I am half mermaid?*

Donovan couldn't help but hear Torey's question in his mind. "Well kid, the good news is that it very well may explain why you never fit in with your peers."

Torey strains his eyes to see into the distance and get a glimpse of his mom, but the air that surrounds his head distorts his view. Donovan realizes Torey's predicament. "Imagine shaping the air around your face like a lens or a window and maybe you will see better."

Torey gives it a try. He imagines scuba goggles and mentally forms the air. It actually seems to be working. He sees a large splash at the ocean's surface.

Donovan presses his now crazed face into Torey's air pocket. "Here comes the filthy bitch now."

The mermaid Leona, a.k.a. the Beachcomber's wife, a.k.a. Torey's mom, gracefully cuts through the water with kicks from her powerful, long tail. She exhibits a goddess-like dynamism over the water. It has been a long time since she has had the opportunity to transform into her true self. She should be overcome with feelings of elation and sheer bliss, but she only feels anger and fear for her little boy.

This is the worst of all possible worst-case scenarios. The dread of not knowing what will happen next and not knowing if there is anything that she can do about it when it does. It fuels a rage in her that makes her both feral and reckless.

Questions assault her livid state of mind. *How could this have happened? How could the demon have gotten so close to my Torey? How could the demon even be here without us becoming aware of its presence?*

She considers that there is much about the demon's nature that she does not know. She wonders if his very presence is what has been making her ill. She damns herself for being too complacent and becoming too relaxed. Now the fate that she has feared for all of these years is upon her and despite all of her training and planning, she feels that she is severely unprepared.

*Oh Zeus, please don't make me go into that hell again,* she prays.

Leona focuses against her blinding rage and feels the rhythm of the currents for signs of her son's whereabouts. Something is unusual. They are moving too quickly. Up ahead a spout of air corkscrews its way to the ocean's depths. But no, it is actually two spouts of air spiraling against each other. There are two beings practicing dynamism! She makes a promise to herself that she will destroy the demon along with any miserable creature that dares to aid it.

Leona does not have the time to proceed cautiously and learn what it is that she is up against like her husband trained her. She has no choice but to swim forward defiantly with her crossbow locked and loaded.

* * *

A constant spray of water frustrates Cassandra's attempts to scan the ocean for signs of Torey and his mother. She can hardly see land anymore and is really concerned for Torey's safety. She yells to be heard through the wind, "Can Torey breathe underwater?"

The Beachcomber yells back, "That would be some trick."

"Did I fall in love with him because..."

"...He is not a mermaid, if that is what you are thinking," he answers, but adds hesitantly, "I don't know. The more time I spend with Leona, the less I feel that I know about mermaids."

"How did you and Torey's mom meet?"

"That, is a long story that is best saved for a better day."

"Well, this is just great." Cassandra frowns, then yells over the roaring engine, "Why is that guy trying to hurt Torey?"

"That is another long story, but that guy is a demon who is using Torey as bait to lure my wife to its hell where she will be trapped forever."

"You're serious?" her voice cracks. For Cassandra, it is second nature to hold her composure, but this is overwhelming. She struggles to keep it together for Torey's sake.

"How do you know where we are going? What are we looking for?"

The Beachcomber points ahead and shouts, "There!"

About two hundred yards away, Mrs. Kilroy breaks the surface. She kicks her powerful tail and skitters along the water like a hooked marlin in order to be sure that her husband sees her location. She lets out a shrill yell that only a mermaid can before she twists and dives back in.

The Beachcomber swings the boat to the left and makes a beeline to Leona's splash before the foam disappears completely. He gets there in time and pulls the throttle into neutral, scanning the sonar screen.

The spectacle that Cassandra just witnessed has momentarily distracted her from her concern for Torey. "That is so freaking awesome."

Then she spots a small vortex swirling on the surface. "Is that a whirlpool?"

The Beachcomber looks to where she is pointing and says, "I am hoping that means that Torey has an air supply." He motions a bit to the left, "There's another one."

Cassandra sees it. "Is that good?"

"It makes no sense to me," he replies.

He checks the sonar screen. "Close to one hundred fathoms." About six hundred feet. This light-colored dot is my wife."

"What is that strange dark splotch?"

"It's either just static on the monitor or it's the gateway to hell."

"Where's the scuba gear?"

"Are you out of your freaking mind? We would be torn apart down there. This is a demon that we are dealing with." He shakes his head with a derisive sneer. "Blondes."

Cassandra is not going to take that. "You are mostly blonde yourself, you crusty old bastard." Before the insults can escalate, she demands, "What is the plan?"

The Beachcomber quickly moves to a compartment at the front of the boat and pulls it open. Inside are three bowling ball-sized iron globes, each connected with an electronic interface. Judging by the strain on his arms as he pulls one out, these things are heavy.

Cassandra has a sinking feeling when she sees them. "Are those…?"

He finishes her sentence. "Depth charges. We are going to blow that son-of-a-bitch back to hell once and for all."

All Cassandra knows is that Torey is somewhere down there and she cannot tell if his father really has a plan, or if he is just plain crazy. Her first wild instinct is to knock him unconscious and… and…and what?

This is crazy. She fully realizes that she has no clue as to what they are up against. She has no choice but to force her mind to calm down for Torey's sake. She resigns herself to settling for complete indecision for now. She will go along with this for a little longer to see how it all plays out.

* * *

Torey looks up at the mermaid that is jetting right for them. *That can't be my mom*, he thinks. She is coming too fast to focus on her despite the "air lens" that he has shaped. He tries frantically to focus, but something else is competing for his attention.

The red glow below them is getting more intense. He looks back and is overcome by a violent feeling of revulsion and fear.

A rusted metal structure coursing with electricity (or something else) frames the entryway to what must be the hell that Donovan talked about. Torey yells in his head, *No. No. I don't belong there!*

He tries to swim frantically upwards to avoid being dragged into it. Every cell in his body is in flight mode.

"Sorry kid, but I can think of no other way. Hey, maybe we will both make it out," Donovan says cheerfully.

Torey gets ready to grab onto a rusty length of the portal, but that electric charge looks like it's going to hurt. He braces himself and grabs tightly onto a twist of steel. To his relief it doesn't burn; it feels cold to the touch. The glowing charge's only effect is to light his skin, like when you put a flashlight in your mouth at night.

He manages to wrap both arms around the metal, but is dismayed by how flimsy the entire construction feels. He holds on for dear life, hoping that his mom can reach him in time. She is so close he can begin to make out the features of her face. *She looks scared.* He tries to ignore the pain in his arms from being scraped against the corroded metal.

A crossbow bolt whizzes past his face and slams into the tentacle that is wrapped around his waist, causing it to lose its grip and let go of Torey. The giant octopus tumbles back into the abyss, pulling Donovan with him.

Torey reaches out for his mom's hand. She's so close.

Just then, Donovan grabs Torey's ankle and forcefully yanks him into the last place that he would ever want to be. Torey immediately feels a mind-numbing pounding in his brain. His vision turns red. He loses his control of his air funnel and is forced to use Donovan's. He can only focus on one thing, his need to breathe. He finally manages to pull his own funnel back, unaware of the three mermaids who are darting in every direction.

Torey can barely form a thought in this terrible place. This hell is assaulting his brain with pounding vibrations. He feels emotions that are unnatural to him: anger and violence, dread and futility. He fights to mentally regain even a simple focus. He resorts to counting in his head, "…forty three, forty four, forty five…" like he used to as a kid when trying to get through a bad session of being teased and bullied. Even that is nearly impossible. The counting becomes replaced with the pulsing of this terrible place, "Boom, boom-boom, boom…"

"MOM!"

Leona belts out a scream of frustration and rage as the trail of blood from her son's scraped arms dissipates. She was so close, but is now too late. She has no choice but to follow him into this hell that she swore she would never go back into. The red glow alone has rendered her almost paralyzed with fear.

For all of their planning for all of these years, she now finds that she does not know what to do. Her mind races with questions that are useless at this point except to delay the inevitability of her going back in there. *How did it get this far? Why didn't Jasper pick up on the signs that the demon was so close? Why didn't we realize that Torey was in trouble?* Leona checks her crossbow and wishes that she had more than this one last bolt. She knows by the two air funnels that the demon is keeping Torey alive to use him as bait. She considers that she might have time to swim up to her husband's boat to get one of his explosives. She could direct the energy of the explosion by using her secondary dynamism over fire. She will poach that evil creep once and for all.

Leona decides on her plan of action and heads back topside with a mighty kick of her tail. As if on cue, one of the air funnels collapses in on itself. It reverts to a soft useless mess of bubbles. Leona gasps at the thought of her baby drowning. Maternal instinct takes over and she darts through the bubbles and into the portal to Donovan's hell. Her only plan now is to move fast and wing it.

* * *

The Beachcomber is the first to notice that one of the whirlpools has disappeared.

"Something is going on. We're down to one whirlpool."

Cassandra watches helplessly as a rush of bubbles percolate the surface where the air funnel was a moment ago. She prays that Torey or parts of Torey do not float up with the bubbles. Meanwhile, Torey's dad is pressing buttons on the panel of the depth charge.

"What are you doing?" Cassandra screams.

He ignores her and consults the sonar screen in order to set the correct depth. She rushes him, trying to knock the charge out of his hands. Torey's father pushes back to keep Cassandra at arm's length, but she accidentally tumbles and lands painfully onto the floor of the boat. As the Beachcomber tries to prevent her fall, the depth charge plops harmlessly into the water without being armed. "What do you think you're doing, you senseless little girl?"

Cassandra is on her back and is sure that he pushed her on purpose. She draws her knife from the holster on her calf and waves the blade in front of her defensively. "You'll kill them, you crazy bastard."

The Beachcomber puts his hands to his head like he has a migraine. He says painfully, as if trying to communicate with a simpleton, "Leona has a thing with fire. She can control it, and direct it, and use it to toast that son of a bitch without letting Torey get even slightly singed."

Cassandra scrambles back to her feet. She still holds the knife, "Isn't there already fire in Hell?"

"Not in this hell. This is a cold watery hell with no warmth to speak of."

Cassandra reads between the lines. "It sounds like you have been there."

"Briefly, but long enough to know that I will not be going back."

The Beachcomber uses the depth finder to re-maneuver the boat back into position over the portal. Out of the corner of his eye, he sees Cassandra throw the holstered knife into the remaining whirlpool hoping against hope that it will somehow get into Torey's hands.

\* \* \*

The unarmed depth charge plummets through the depths towards the portal and gets caught up as it settles down, trapped between the construct of the portal and a rocky outcropping. Its LED screen flashes impotently. The knife, however, spins through the air funnel like a branch in a tornado and makes it through the portal.

\* \* \*

Leona charges through the cavern urging a tidal force of water before her. She must keep the demon off balance and on the defensive. The force of water stirs up all of the debris in the place and slams the hulls of the old ships into each other. All of the tidy order that Donovan had worked so hard to achieve over the past decades is thrown into turmoil. The pulsing rage and pain from the red glow instantly increases.

Somewhere, Donovan screams out in rage.

Leona's state of mind is quickly becoming fragile and she can no longer trust her perceptions. She is losing her cool as the pulsating vibes of this hell take a toll on her state of mind. Leona knows that she must be hallucinating. She sees the shadows of mermaids swimming with a bizarre stop-motion effect created by the flashing lights. Her reason tells her that there can be no other mermaids here. Not in this place.

*There.* Her skin crawls at the sight of the demon holding Torey in front of him. Torey is bug-eyed as he struggles to not inhale water. The air funnel has been pulled away from him. The bastard is daring her to take a shot at him, thinking that Torey will drown without him providing oxygen. The arrogant bastard is even pretending not to look at her.

Leona squeezes the trigger. She can take care of her son without his help.

Donovan ducks suddenly as the crossbow bolt zooms straight for his head.

One of the mermaids rushes forward to protect Donovan. The bolt impales her hand. A cloud of blood flows from her wound. *Why is a mermaid protecting this beast?*

Donovan commands the octopus. "Take her." The octopus stirs, but does not make a move for Leona. He commands again. "She's here. Take her and set me free."

The entire cavern rumbles with a massive explosion as the

Beachcomber's second depth charge blows near the portal. Leona reacts quickly and pulls the fire into the cavern. She directs it at Donovan close enough to burn him without harming her son.

The octopus darts forward past the fire, swooshing past Leona and jetting towards the portal. The giant creature slows only enough to maneuver itself through the tattered portal without further damaging it. Once out of the chamber, it propels upwards to confront its attackers.

Donovan screams through the pain of his seared body. "You missed her! Get back here you filthy beast!"

Donovan is defenseless against Leona without his harpoon, but a knife in a holster tumbles through the debris and into his reach. He snatches it despite the extreme pain of the seared left side of his torso. He cannot die in this place, but he can feel pain.

He is not about to give up. He might very well die from his wounds once free, but his desire to get out of this hell is stronger than the pain of his charred flesh.

The explosion has taken a toll on the structural stability of the portal. Huge ornate columns begin to crumble. Stones rain down from the trembling marble carvings of heathen gods.

Donovan smacks the side of Torey's face to snap him out of his stupor. "You are on your own, kid. Do you hear me? You have to take control of this."

He abandons his focus from the air stream that immediately twists away from Torey. Torey struggles to focus and regain control of the air spout.

Donovan turns his full attention on killing Leona.

* * *

Cassandra watches as a white cloud from the explosion rushes to the surface. She feels helpless and seriously questions if her presence here is doing any good at all. She is terrified to see what might float up, yet she watches despite herself. She prays that no human or mermaid body parts will surface. She glances at the old man, and sees that he is arming the third depth charge. She quickly looks back to the water as she spots a dark shape amongst the white bubbles. She leans out for a closer look.

"What is that?"

The water explodes as a tangle of giant tentacles burst through. They grab at the boat with rows of powerful suckers and tilt it dangerously forward. Cassandra screams as she tumbles towards the face of the creature. The Beachcomber grabs her by the wrist with one hand and pulls her back up to the boat's console. The creature is trying to capsize the boat.

"Shoot it!" he yells frantically.

Cassandra wraps her legs around the chair's post to secure herself, then leans out with her pistol to get a clean shot, but the octopus is quick and one of its tentacles deftly snatches the gun from her hand. The pistol falls into the ocean.

She grabs at the AR15 that dangles from its strap on the pilot's seat. She yells to the Beachcomber, "Where is the safety?"

The Beachcomber fends off a tentacle with point blank shots of a pistol. "There is no safety."

Cassandra squeezes the trigger, but is not ready for the kick. A spray of bullets harmlessly shoots into the sky. She loses her grip and her second gun drops overboard. *It looks so easy on television!*

The Beachcomber is still shooting methodically at the tentacles one shot at a time as he manages to cradle the third depth charge with his other arm. "Shoot its head."

"I think the octopus' head is under the boat," Cassandra shouts back, "and I think there are two of them because I count at least ten arms."

"It is just the one and it's not an octopus. It's a demon. Just shoot it!"

*Demon!* Cassandra looks frantically for another weapon. She is relieved that the tentacles seem to be reaching for the old man, but she is wise enough to know that it will take the both of them to survive this. She feels helpless to do anything, and out of desperation, she grabs the rope that is attached to the anchor and does her best to tangle it around and tie two of its tentacles together.

Torey's dad is squeezing off round after round point blank into the demon's grabbing appendages, shouting at it like a madman in a peculiar language.

Cassandra uses the rest of the rope to tangle one of the injured tentacles with the two others that she has already wrapped. She heaves the anchor overboard, but it does little to stop the octopus' assault. The octopus does, however, make a grab for her and wraps a tentacle around her midriff.

* * *

Torey's mom has Donovan's knife-wielding wrist in one hand and is trying to tear at his ugly face with her other. One of the mermaids is trying to pull her away from him while the other two are trying to pull Donovan away from Leona. She still doesn't believe they are real, but rather some cruel hallucination created by Donovan. The mermaids keep yelling ridiculous things at her like, "Don't hurt him," and "Hasn't he suffered enough?" and "Don't do this!"

*This makes no sense!*

There is no time to think or to make sense of everything that is happening. Leona must fight against the hallucinations and get her son out of this hell before the portal completely gives way and they are trapped here forever.

Leona lets go of Donovan's wrist then splinters his old surfboard with a swipe of her tail. The two mermaids drag him away from her.

A car-sized chunk of one of the ancient columns falls between Donovan and the two mermaids. One of the mermaids takes a hard hit to her head and the other is pinned by her tail between the column and the hull of an old wooden ship.

Out of desperation, Leona tries mind speaking to her son and is surprised when they connect. "I need you to swim to the portal."

Torey replies, "But…"

She cuts him off. "Swim. Now."

Torey can't make sense of the chaos around him, but he can mentally focus on swimming, though it causes his focus on his air supply to become shaky. It begins to shrivel.

Leona grabs her son by the band of his shorts to hurry his alarmingly slow pace.

Torey can barely even concentrate, but by some bizarre distraction in his mind he notices that his mom is giving him a wedgie. Since he no longer needs to swim for himself, he tries to reestablish his air supply.

Suddenly Donovan desperately grabs onto Torey's ankle. The extra weight slows down Leona's progress, but she continues to pull upwards. One of the other mermaids takes Torey's arm and tries to help pull him towards the portal.

Torey hears Donovan's panicked voice in his head. "I can't stay here. No no no! I can't be here any longer!"

"You are not going to kill my mother!" Torey yells in

his head.

"I have to. I have to kill her! The demon didn't take her! You can kill her! She is right there. We can kill her together!"

Donovan swings up his legs and scissor-wraps Leona's tail to prevent her escape.

Leona shrieks with rage and lets go of her son. She must trust the other mermaid to get him out, but she must first break Donovan's grip from Torey's ankle.

All four of them drift downward, as the weight is too much for the one mermaid to bear by herself.

Donovan tightens his grip for all he's worth. He knows that this is his last chance to get out of this hell and leave the stinking mermaid here, the one who condemned him here in the first place. He tightens his grip on the knife with his free hand.

Leona lets go of Torey so she can confront this demon face-to-face for the last time. She locks eyes with him and gets ready to tear his arm off to save her son.

Donovan finally has her within his reach, within his knife's reach. *This is it!*

He hesitates.

Maybe he is still susceptible to her mermaid charms, or maybe he realizes that he still loves her, but for whatever reason, he hesitates. His hesitation is long enough for Torey to get a glimpse of the knife.

"Mom," Torey yells and his mind reacts more from reflex than by conscious effort. He releases his concentration from his air funnel, which quickly pulls away from him and dissipates. He channels dynamism over earth into pulling a serpentine column of sand from the floor and sends it pounding into Donovan's midsection.

Donovan loses his grip from Torey's ankle as he is pile-driven by a ton of wet sand and slammed into a stone column. The impact rolls the column just enough to free the pinned mermaid, who is in obvious pain.

The chaotic currents flowing through the water stir up the remains of centuries' worth of sunken ships, downed warplanes and skulls and bones. The ordered stacks of the detritus of battle are scattered to better reflect the pandemonium from whence they came.

Disorder reigns in this dismal corner of hell once again. The red glow that had once only seeped from the dark crannies of this place has grown to an all-consuming presence. The red is everywhere, and it pulses with all encompassing intensity.

"Why didn't you tell me that you have a dynamism over earth?" Torey hears the words from his mentor, his friend, his enemy, that are full of pain and despair. Torey feels a twinge of guilt, but is too busy fighting against his oxygen-starved lungs' reflex to suck in water to let it strike home.

His mother and the other mermaid continue to rush to get him to the portal. Torey knows that they will make it, but he is too exhausted to pull down another air funnel. He knows that he will not surface in time to catch another breath.

A feeling of calm overtakes his senses as he comes to terms with his imminent demise. Torey looks back and sees the two injured mermaids struggling to carry and pull Donovan to the portal.

Pain and desperation are written over all of their faces. He is certain that despite the mermaids' pain and wounds, they could certainly make it out of the chamber in time, yet they continue the struggle to save Donovan. It strikes him as being the saddest event that he has witnessed in his young life.

Torey knows by the sudden release of pressure inside of his

head that they have made it back through the portal. He is relieved that he will not die in that horrid place. A gasp of salt water burns his lungs. He has no air left to cough it back out.

He knows that his last memory of this life will be watching Donovan and the two mermaids, their faces bathed in a hellish red glow, screaming as the portal crumbles and cuts off their last hopes of escape.

# Chapter 18

# *Swimming With A Limp*

Leona is still confused as to how one of the mermaids who she was sure was a hallucination swims through the portal. Now that they are away from the hellish red light and brain-numbing pounding, she recognizes her. *How can it be?*

It is her sister Sirena! A million questions arise, but will have to wait to be asked. They swim upwards towards a full out battle at the surface. Through the murky depths she can just make out the thrashing of the demon octopus and the crazy upright position of her husband's boat. She feels Torey's body go limp as he loses consciousness.

Her crimson-haired sister takes Torey's head with both hands and pulls him to her until they are face to face. She kisses his lips tenderly and lovingly until she feels him return the kiss.

Torey's eyes snap open, fully alert. He is still deep underwater and he can breathe; or rather, he doesn't feel the need to breathe.

Despite his relief and his second chance at life, his first thought is how is he going to explain to Cassandra that he is married to this mermaid who saved his life with a kiss.

A sudden explosion knocks all such thoughts from his mind. A depth charge has exploded between them and the boat. Leona uses her dynamism to arc the blast around them at the portal to collapse it once and for all.

The octopus charges past them and follows the fire into the portal just as the depth charge that was previously wedged against it unexpectedly explodes. The portal's utter destruction is absolute. All signs that it or the cavern beneath it existed are gone. Nothing is left but rippled sand.

The force of the blasts hits the group hard. Torey is pulled away from the others. His body is buffeted from all sides as if he were going over the falls of the world's largest wave.

* * *

Cassandra falls back hard into the boat. The beast and its sinewy tentacles that were tightly wrapped around her waist suddenly withdraw and disappear below the surface.

"Yes!" Torey's dad yells ecstatically. "We must have destroyed the portal."

Cassandra can't believe what she is hearing. "They are still down there! Torey is still down there!"

"They're probably alright," he replies sullenly.

* * *

The washing machine effect of the turbulent water finally settles down, but a loud ringing in Torey's ears remains. He is completely disoriented and cannot tell which way is up and which way is down. He has no air bubbles to help him determine which way to go. He decides to swim as best as he can manage, if only to do something besides just float here.

Leona grabs Torey by his ankle and pulls him in the opposite direction from where he is swimming. She points her finger upwards and winks at him. Her playful wink acts to release some of the tension. Torey reverses his direction. He breaks a huge grin and hugs his mother with a mighty bear hug. They are still fifty yards under water.

* * *

The sun is low in the sky and Cassandra can't believe that the Beachcomber is actually bailing water out of the damaged boat with a hand pump instead of looking for his wife and son. She shields her eyes with her hands and prays that she can find Torey and that somehow he is still alive, but no matter which way she looks, all she sees is empty water.

A tear trickles down her check. She promises that Torey's stupid reckless father will pay dearly if he has killed them.

"NO!" She grabs a rifle and throws it as hard as she can down against the water.

"Hey!" A familiar voice says.

"OhmyGodohmyGodohmyGod!" Cassandra yells, jumping into the water and into Torey's arms. She frantically kisses his face as he coughs and tries to get used to breathing air again.

"You made it! I knew you would make it!"

Torey's brain is still numb from the beating it took. When he finally catches his breath he asks, "Are you blonde?"

Her laughter is full of relief, and joy, and love. "Do you like it?"

"Does this mean I can call you Cassie?" Torey teases.

She grins. "Not a chance, fish boy."

Torey can only smile and tells her, "I love you."

Cassandra wants to tell him she loves him too, but is leery of the feral stare that his mom is laying on her.

Torey's mom is also brain-addled when she surfaces in time to hear this exchange. Leona wonders about this young girl who has stolen her little boy's heart. She tells her husband, "Get me out of this water, will you."

The beachcomber slips his arms under her armpits and pulls her up until she rests what would be her butt on the rail of the boat. She twists and flops her tail into the boat. "Why is *she* here?"

He shrugs. "It's a long story. Climb aboard you two, help me towel off your mother."

Neither Torey nor Cassandra is ready for how quickly his mother would revert back to human form. One moment they are toweling her off when suddenly gallons of water flood the deck of the boat and her tail shrivels and morphs back into a pair of legs. The scales and red colorations fade almost as quickly back to normal skin tones.

"That is too cool." Cassandra says, before asking, "So if we dumped you back into the water your tail would grow back, right?"

Leona doesn't know what to think of this brash young woman. "Do you have a mother?"

"Oh, you cannot tell my mother about any of this. She would go ballistic if she knew what I was up to."

This causes Leona and the Beachcomber to exchange glances. Leona asks her husband, "Can this one be trusted?"

"She is bull-headed and belligerent and a force of nature by her own right, but yes, I believe that she can be trusted."

"Cassandra, I trust that you realize what you have gotten yourself into and it is certainly nice to meet you." She kisses

Cassandra's cheek, and then tells her husband, "Can this heap get us back home?"

It takes Torey's dad a few tries to turn over the engine, but it does catch. The engine sputters and coughs as they start to move.

Cassandra breathes a sigh of relief. The last thing she needs is more drama today.

They all turn their heads as a loud shriek catches their attention. Off the starboard side, a mermaid breaks the surface and tail-dances across the water before disappearing again. Both Cassandra and the Beachcomber exclaim, "What the hell!"

They all look at where the foam from the splash is quickly fading to see if she will resurface. The mermaid surprises them by jumping into the boat from the port side. She slithers in and makes herself at home right on Torey's lap.

Torey is stunned. He doesn't know what to think or how to react. How will he explain this to Cassandra? The mermaid who saved Torey's life gazes into his eyes and moves in to kiss his lips.

As if Cassandra would ever let this happen. She intercepts the kiss by sliding her hand between their two sets of lips.

"Oh no you don't," she warns.

Torey's mom laughs. "It's okay, she's his Aunt Sirena."

The mermaid says something in a mermaid helium-burp-sounding language, and then snatches a kiss on Torey's lips despite Cassandra's objections.

Cassandra rolls her eyes at Torey. "You have the strangest family ever."

Torey's family has never been more than just he and his mom and dad. He is glad for the new addition, even if she is part fish. He sighs tiredly and says, "Tell me about it."

The rest of the ride home is mostly quiet and awkward. Although everyone on the boat has a million questions, they all find themselves too exhausted to speak. For now they are content to just let the sun set quietly behind them.

# Epilogue

*It has been my experience that once your life turns wierd, good luck trying to get it back to normal. It doesn't seem that my head will ever feel right after all of that red pulsing that it took in Donovan's hell. I sometimes feel like I am outside of my body and watching myself like a stranger. There are still so many unanswered questions, but I will tell you what I know.*

*The ride back home that day was slow and awkward as my dad struggled to keep his seriously damaged boat sputtering along. It felt like forever until we got back to land. We all had a million questions that needed to be answered, but we were all too exhausted to ask them. And my leg was going numb from the weight of my aunt sitting on my lap.*

*My dad didn't think to bring an extra wrap, so while my mom was covered up like a civilized person, my aunt sat on my lap in all her naked glory. It would take a long time for her transformation from mermaid to human because all of the towels were already soaked from drying off my mom.*

*I could tell that Cassandra wasn't too thrilled with the seating arrangements, but she seemed preoccupied by something else. She kept staring at my dad like she was trying to figure something out about him. By then I knew her enough to know that she didn't trust him and that something went down between them while they were looking for us.*

*Days later, my dad told me that Cassandra has bigger cajones than some of the soldiers that he had fought with in the war, and that I had no idea what I was getting into as far as dating her. This confused me, but if she can deal with my family, then I can certainly deal with her big cajones.*

*Back on the boat, I also noticed that my dad and my aunt were exchanging their own suspicious looks. It was like they were both expecting the other to attack at any moment, but they just met, so I couldn't figure it out. I heard the jokes about in-laws not liking each other, so maybe that's what it was. It occurred to me that my dad has secrets of his own and is in many ways as mysterious as my mom. Anyway, like I said, I was really tired so I wasn't able to think clearly.*

*My mom was pretty quiet too. After she asked how I learned to use dynamism and I told her that Donovan taught me, she just sat there with a haunted look on her face. She was no longer the glorious mermaid, strong and powerful. She was plain old mom again. And when she would glance at her sister, the best that she could manage was a weak smile, like she was confused and felt guilty about something. It makes me wonder, now that I think of it, if those other two mermaids who are trapped with Donovan are also related to us.*

*Poor Donovan. Oddly enough, I still think of him as a friend even though he tried to kill my mom. And I don't think that he is a demon — a lost soul maybe, but not a demon. My family was never religious and now I can sort of understand why with my mom being half fish and all, but I started saying prayers for Donovan. I don't really know how to pray, but I figure positive wishes are a good place to start. I wonder sometimes if I will ever see him again.*

*I didn't actually realize that we were nearing the shore until I followed my aunt's eager gaze. There was stupid Dillon pacing on the beach like an excited puppy. I still wonder how he knew that the love of his life, the mermaid who kissed him at the surf competition, was on the boat with us. We were still pretty far out, but there he was wading into the water.*

*My aunt was finally completely dry and was flexing her legs and trying to get used to them. She looked young like a teenager, but, I found out later she is really like, four-hundred years old. My mom is the younger of the two and is only about two-hundred years old. What a mind freak.*

*We were all totally startled when Aunt Sirena jumped up off my damp lap and dove overboard into the water. This was my first time actually seeing a mermaid transform. The way the water and air lit up with purple-colored arcs of plasma and flashes of green phosphorescence was spectacular against the darkening sky. I've seen it many times since, but the show is always best at night, and it fully reinforces my confidence in the supernatural and dynamism.*

*Anyway, she swam straight to Dillon and I am not sure but I think that I heard him squeal like a little girl when he rushed to meet her. They were still making out in the water when we finally reached the beach. My mom shook her head and said that they appeared to be fully bonded and as good as married.*

*And that is how the longest day of my life ended.*

*Like I said, you can't ever get things back to normal once it goes weird, but we tried. We went back to school like our lives had never changed. Of course, Cassandra blew everyone's minds with her natural blonde hair and new surfer-girl look. She is now, hands down, the hottest girl in school, but I think that it has as much to do with her personality as it does her physical appearance.*

*At first when the mean girls and the cheerleaders, and even the goths, tried and failed to claim her as part of their own cliques, they tried to hate on her. She didn't join any of the cliques, but instead was cool to everyone, whether they liked her back or not. Even Byron tried to hate the new Cassandra, but who is he kidding? Since he became the kicker of the football team and wears a jersey on game day and is dating a pom-pom girl, it was only a matter of time before he became a bit less uptight. Cassandra and Byron are really good friends again.*

*The Appalling Twins still think that a fish ate my mother, and they are still not the friendliest kids in school, but they don't bully kids too much anymore. They spend most of their free time training to be lifeguards and taking EMT classes. Go figure.*

*Cassandra comes over a lot after school. She is obsessed with my mom and aunt and they are trying to teach her about dynamism. It is hard for humans to grasp the concept, but once you see dynamism in action and realize that it really does exist, it becomes a little easier. She is obviously not as strong with it as my mom or my aunt, or even me because I am only half human, but it is pretty cool to watch her when she gets a flame to jump from a match and dance across her fingertips. And I'm glad to have someone to talk to about it. Her other dynamism is over water, which I totally envy. Her surfing abilities are going to be world class by next summer.*

*Cassandra was concerned that being the son of a mermaid gave me powers to enchant her to fall in love with me, but the truth is, she has totally enchanted me. I am hopelessly in love with her and I couldn't be happier.*

*My mom and aunt never seem to have a free moment together as my dad is always hovering around nearby. He doesn't bother to patrol the beach anymore, looking for something that might tip him off that Donovan is nearby. He says it will be a long time before another portal can be constructed. I don't know how he knows this, but the point is he has a lot of free time on his hands and nothing to do. He's kind of driving us all nuts. And Aunt Sirena really hates his guts.*

*Aunt Sirena feels uncomfortable in the house, so much so that she sleeps outside in the ocean. Oh, and get this, Dillon — I will never call him Uncle Dillon — comes over all the time and even spends the night with my Aunt. And he sleeps with her underwater. What a freak!*

# Chapter 19

## *So I Lied*
## *There's One More Chapter*

A crescent moon smiles down from a cloudless spring sky. It is after midnight and all is quiet at the Kilroy house. Down at the beach at the water's edge, however, all hell is breaking loose.

Sirena thrashes about in the water, clearly in pain. Leona is right there with her trying to keep her comfortable. A green phosphorescent glow surrounds them. Sirena is giving birth to her and Dillon's child in the ocean.

Dillon is as pale as a fish's underbelly, freaking out. "How am I going to explain this to my parents!"

The Beachcomber tries to distract him. "Dillon, listen to me. We need hot washcloths. Go to the house and boil some water."

Dillon knows enough to not trust Mr. Kilroy after the "dip flush" incident. He isn't going to fall for it this time.

"Dude, you have to be strong," Cassandra tells him. "Get in there and hold Sirena's hand."

That is actually bad advice because being next to Sirena is probably the most dangerous place to be at the moment, but Dillon does as he's told.

"Is this how I was born?" Torey questions his dad.

"No, I already told you. You were born in the bathtub."

The unearthly glow of phosphorous amps up into an almost blinding glare. Blue and orange flashes of plasma arc from around Sirena's midsection. The water boils and steams around her.

"It's time!" Leona yells out. "Torey and Cassandra get yourselves in here."

"This is sick," Cassandra exclaims as she wades into the unnaturally warm and strangely colorful roiling water.

Torey follows behind her. "What do you need us to do?"

"Get Dillon out of here," his mom yells.

Dillon has passed out and Sirena is trying to keep his head from sinking below the water as she is struggling to give birth. Cassandra is closest to Dillon so she grabs him under his armpits and drags him to shore with the assistance of Torey holding his ankles.

Sirena shrieks out in pain with her natural mermaid voice. Her body contracts violently as she writhes into and out of a fetal position. She belts out a scream that must surely be heard for miles.

Once the scream subsides, Torey's mom holds up a wiggly baby mermaid by its aqua blue and orange tail. Her big green eyes are already open and alert as she takes in her surroundings.

Leona directs Torey. "Hold your niece while I tend to your aunt. Her name is Tempestia."

"Tempestia? Is that good?"

Torey does as he is told and grabs his niece with one hand clutching the tail as his mother was doing, but uses his other arm to cradle her. He tells Cassandra, "Wake up stupid Dillon. He should be holding this squiggler."

Leona lifts her sister's head up from under the water as her shrieks of pain turn into tired giggles and relieved laughter. The two mermaids hug each other for a job well done.

Dillon has regained consciousness again and stumbles back into the water to where Torey stands.

"Here, hold your baby."

He reaches to hand the mermaid baby over to her father, but before he can make the handoff, Tempestia giggles and squiggles in his grasp. Torey tries his best to juggle and keep hold of her, but is unable to. His niece plops into the water and the inexplicable happens.

The baby swims off like a shot to deeper waters, a red and orange glow still visible for the first hundred yards before fading.

Sirena looks at Torey with an open-mouthed silent, "Why?" As exhausted as she is, she dives into the next wave and gives chase.

Leona commands her husband. "Get the boat and follow us."

She disappears beneath the water and chases after her sister.

The Beachcomber is not happy.

"This is not good!" he yells to the sky. Then he yells for Torey and Cassandra and Dillon to help him with the boat.

Dillon stands in the dark water, dumbfounded.

Cassandra waits for Torey, who still stands in the water staring at the spot where he dropped the baby. He takes a moment to ponder the events of this past year and his rise from nerd to becoming the coolest kid in Dick Dale High. Maybe Donovan was right all those months ago about cool being unsustainable, because at this very moment, Torey feels like the biggest tool in the shed.

~ The End ~